'68

'68

A Novel

BY C.W. SPOONER

iUniverse, Inc.
Bloomington

'68
A Novel

iUniverse books may be ordered through booksellers or by contacting:

iUniverse
1663 Liberty Drive
Bloomington, IN 47403
www.iuniverse.com
1-800-Authors (1-800-288-4677)

ISBN: 978-1-4620-7316-0 (sc)
ISBN: 978-1-4620-7317-7 (ebk)

Printed in the United States of America

iUniverse rev. date: 12/18/2011

Dedication

For the Spooner kids—Kim, Cheryl, Matt, Rachel, and Gabe—who make me proud every day.

New Year's Eve, 1967

THEY WATCHED THE IMAGE ON the television screen, the lighted ball dropping in Times Square. "Five . . . four . . . three . . . two . . . one . . . Happy New Year!" The lucky ones turned to that special someone and shared a sweet kiss.

"Happy New Year, babe. I love you."

"I love you too."

"I wonder what this year will bring? All good things, I hope."

"Yeah, well, we got that damn war. Maybe that will wind down."

"And we've got to elect a president."

"Oh, I think old LBJ has a lock on that one."

"Maybe. We'll see."

"You know, some years just come and go and you never even notice. You never remember what happened. Like 1965, or 1966. Came and went, nothing much to remember."

"Well, Aunt Tillie died in '65. And little Jethro was born in '66."

"Yeah, but I mean in the big picture, world events. Like, you'll always remember 1963, November 22, where you were, what you were doing when you heard the news from Dallas. But most years just come and go. Know what I mean?"

"Yes, I know what you mean. And you know what? This party is a bore. What say we go home, take off our clothes and get in a pile?"

"Now you're talking. Start the year with a bang. Great idea!"

"I'll get my coat and we'll say goodbye."

There is a theory that used to be taught in college communications courses. I goes something like this: each of us lives in our own personal box, like a big refrigerator box, and the only way you can look out at the world is through a lens on one side. That lens is made up of everything that has ever happened to you: the good, the bad, and the ugly. It is colored by all the people who have touched your life: parents, family members, friends, teachers, and coworkers. Most of it is complete by the time you are an adolescent, but it can change as things happen to you, what the theorists call Significant Emotional Events. We can talk about other influences—the town where you live, the neighborhood where you grew up, what you do for a living—because they all shape the way you look at the world.

It all goes into your lens.

Let's consider a few hypothetical questions. If you served in World War II and came under enemy fire and saw your buddies die, how would you view the conflict in Vietnam and the anti-war protests all around the country? If you grew up in a strictly segregated community, where *those people* rode in the back of the bus and drank from separate water fountains, how would you view the relentless push for civil rights? If you believed in the rule of law and the genius of our constitutional system of government "Of the People, By the People, For the People," how would you view the successive waves of urban riots and assassinations? How would these events appear through your lens, and would it be changed by what you saw?

This is the story of several families living in a small town in Northern California. Each family has its lens, and each family member has his or her personal variation. We'll see how those lenses are affected during the course of a single year as some Significant Emotional Events unfold. Are there significant changes, and are they for the good? Do people really change and grow?

Well, that is for you to decide.

Getting back to our New Year's Eve couple, they were right of course: most years come and go and are, to paraphrase Mr. Lincoln, *little noted nor long remembered.* This one—1968—would not be one of those years.

Sunday, January 14

T HE CROWD STARTED ARRIVING AT Skip's Place around 11:00 AM. By kickoff time, it was two-deep at the bar and every table out on the floor was occupied. Skip Marks wasn't surprised. It was Super Bowl Sunday, the Oakland Raiders vs. the Green Bay Packers in Super Bowl II, and Vallejo, California, was close enough to Oakland to bask in the glow. The silver and black excitement was so thick you could reach out and touch it.

Skip and his wife Marty had worked hard getting ready for this day. Bowls of chips, dip, pretzels, and popcorn were placed on the bar and at each of the tables. At the half, they would cover the pool table carefully to protect against spills, and then put out a lunch spread that would be remembered fondly in the days to come: cold cuts, cheeses, pickles, breads, potato salad, and Marty's special macaroni salad with tiny bay shrimp. Finally, an assortment of cookies, cakes, and pies would hit the pool table. If a customer went away hungry, it was strictly by choice.

Two bartenders worked the bar with Skip while Marty directed the three-person wait staff. It was all they could do to keep up with the drink orders. The staff would see very little of the game itself, able to glance up only on occasion to one of the television sets mounted around the room.

A huge cheer went up with the kickoff. Groans followed a couple of field goals by the Packers' Don Chandler. Then, in the second quarter, Bart Starr connected on a pass to Boyd Dowler.

"Oh no . . . get him . . . get him! Tackle that sonofabitch!"

The play went for sixty-two yards and a touchdown, the Packers led 13-0, and some of the excitement left the room. Then, the Raiders launched a drive that ended with a twenty-two yard touchdown pass, Daryl Lamonica to Bill Miller, and suddenly the excitement was back.

"We're in this, baby! We're in it!"

The glow diminished slightly when Chandler hit another field goal just before the half.

They put out the lunch spread at halftime and the pool table was mobbed. Marty's macaroni salad was gone in a flash, and the staff had to replenish the bread and cold cuts several times. Skip did a quick check of the cash registers and saw that this was already the highest volume day in the history of Skip's Place.

The third quarter started with high anticipation. Then came an eighty-two yard drive by Green Bay that ended with a two yard touchdown run. The highlight was a thirty-five yard pass to Max McGee, the final reception of his career.

"Oh no, not McGee! Not that old fart!"

Then Chandler kicked another field goal that made it 26-7, and some of the patrons headed for the door. The fourth quarter was just underway when Herb Adderly picked off a Lamonica pass and ran it back sixty yards for a touchdown. Just a handful of customers hung on until the bitter end. The final score was 33-14. The Packers had earned another championship trophy and they carried Vince Lombardi off the field on their shoulders. Only a half-dozen cookies were left on the pool table.

It took a while to clean up the place and dispose of all the trash. Finally, Skip dismissed the extra help and he and Marty sat down with a cold bottle of beer.

Marty proposed a toast: "Here's to a happy, healthy, and prosperous 1968."

"I'll drink to that. And here's to Pete Rozelle."

They clinked bottles and smiled across the little table.

Happy. Healthy. Prosperous. Skip pondered Marty's toast as he went about closing out the cash register. She could have added *continued.* Continued health, happiness, and prosperity. Things had certainly gone well for them since they purchased the bar in 1962. He and Marty were newlyweds then, and it had proved to be a great partnership. He watched her now, busy restocking the cold case, and he smiled. Who knew you could meet your soul mate working behind the jewelry counter at the City of Paris department store?

He was visiting his Aunt Ruth Lev that weekend in April of 1962, and he'd gone to the City of Paris in downtown Vallejo to look for a gift for his favorite aunt. The pretty girl at the counter selected a lovely brooch and handed it to him to inspect. He asked the price and when she gave him the answer, he mumbled that it was crazy, using the Yiddish word *meshugeh.*

She smiled at him and said, "So, you're Jewish?"

"Yes. Yes, I am."

"Me too," she replied, and smiled at him again. It was then that he noticed the shiny black hair streaming down over her shoulders and those lovely green eyes.

Three months later they were married in Aunt Ruthie's beautiful garden, and shortly thereafter, they purchased the bar that would become Skip's Place. It was down on the waterfront, at the foot of Georgia Street, a popular spot for shipyard workers and for sailors heading to town on shore leave. Skip had a vision of a clean, well-lighted place where you could bring your wife or your best girl and feel at home. That's exactly what he and Marty had created, and business was good.

The saloon business was a natural for Skip. His father ran a couple of successful watering holes in San Francisco, a notoriously thirsty town. Skip literally grew up in the business. But it was a long and winding road that brought the Marks family to California, stretching back through stops in Chicago and New York City.

Morris Marks, Skip's father, had seen the ominous handwriting on the walls in their native Germany in the early thirties. He made arrangements to take his bride and immigrate to America, counseling his parents, brothers, and sisters to do the same. Sheldon, immediately tagged with the nickname Skip, was born in San Francisco in 1934.

Aside from Morris's little family unit, only his sister Ruth survived the Holocaust. Morris brought Ruth to San Francisco after the war where she met and eventually married a widower named Asher Lev. The Levs settled in Vallejo where Asher prospered in the banking business. In 1950, Asher's son Bradley and daughter-in-law Esther became parents of a baby boy they named Milton Jacob, and Ruth and Asher settled comfortably into the roles of *Bubbe* and *Zayde*. When Asher died suddenly in 1957, Bradley stepped in to run the business. Ruth was left with a lovely home and a secure income.

Skip glanced at Marty, finished now with the restocking chores. They had not been blessed with children and they'd come to accept that fact of their life. But, they were still crazy (he should say *meshugeh*) in love with each other. He'd have to remember to thank Aunt Ruthie for settling in Vallejo.

Saturday, January 20

J OHN HARRIS WAS ENGAGED IN his favorite Saturday morning activity: working in his backyard garden. His winter vegetables were doing well, thanks to the mild Bay Area weather. He hoed and weeded and pruned where necessary, and thought about whether or not to add compost for moisture control and to protect the delicate roots. This was therapy for John after a grueling week on the shipyard.

His friends called him "Big John," and for good reason. It wasn't that he was tall—perhaps six feet two on a good day—but rather it was the bulk and the impression of strength that he projected. He weighed in at two hundred and forty pounds and he carried it with an athletic grace that made you think he could suit up and play offensive guard for the local semi-pro football team.

As John continued his gardening, he noticed the compact figure of a man wearing a broad-brimmed straw hat working steadily in his neighbor's yard. The low picket fence that surrounded the property made it easy to see what was going on in your neighbor's domain. John wondered what Bart West, his neighbor, was up to. The figure moving about briskly—spading, hoeing, and raking—wasn't old man West. He must have hired a gardener for this project, whatever it was. But why now, when he had the house up for sale? Finally, John couldn't stand the suspense any longer. He walked over to the back fence and called out to the man in the hat.

"Hey there . . . can you come over for a second?" The man looked up, hesitated for a moment, and then walked over to the fence, removing his work gloves as he approached. "Hi, I'm John Harris. What are you working on there?" John saw that the short, powerfully built man was Japanese.

"Hi, I'm Ken Hashimoto." He gave John a firm handshake. "I'm building a rock garden."

"Well, I'll be damned! Why would old West want a rock garden? Especially now, when he's got the place up for sale?"

"It's not for Mr. West." Ken gave a slight smile. "I bought the place. We just moved in. It's nice to meet you, John."

John was dumbstruck for a moment. West had sold the house, he was gone, his new neighbor was a Jap, and he was building a damn rock garden! He backed away from the conversation without ever saying *welcome to the neighborhood*. A few minutes later, he was washing his hands in the kitchen sink and looking to his wife for answers.

"So, what the hell is going on? West sold the house? To a Jap? Why didn't I know about this?"

Martha Harris patted her husband's back and tried to reassure him. "The Wests sold the house late last month. They're gone, relocated to San Diego to be close to their kids."

"And they sold to a damn Jap?"

"Japanese, John. Don't use the word 'Jap'."

"I'll use any dang word I want! Did you know this was happening?"

"Of course. June West was a good neighbor and a friend." Martha was puttering around her kitchen, getting ready to prepare dinner.

"But, Japs in our neighborhood? What the hell was West thinking?"

"Now, John. They're just people, just like us."

"Just like us, hell! We lost a lot of good men to those little bastards. A lot of good men, Martha. I know; I was there."

"I know you were, honey. But Ken Hashimoto wasn't. Actually, I think Tami said they're from Santa Clara."

"Oh, so now it's Ken and Tami, is it?"

"Yes, I met her the other day. I brought her a cake. She seems very nice. You know, their son is John Jr.'s age. He plays baseball. They'll be teammates this year on the varsity team."

John stood at the sink scowling, looking out the window toward his neighbor's house. He could see a figure moving about in the kitchen window, a woman with short black hair.

"Well . . . I'll be damned," was all he could muster.

Kenji Hashimoto leaned against the kitchen counter, shuffling some bills that had arrived in the mail that day. "I met our neighbor today—John Harris. What a piece of work!"

"What do you mean by that?" Tami was moving quickly around the kitchen, preparing the evening meal.

"I mean he thought I was the Wests' gardener. You should have seen the look on his face when I told him we bought the place."

"Oh, I'm sure you are exaggerating. Martha Harris brought over a nice cake and we visited for a while. She seems very nice."

"Oh really? You think it's safe to eat the damn cake? Maybe we should give a little to the dog first."

"Stop it now, Kenji. I'm sure they are nice people. Their son is Eric's age. They'll be teammates this year at the high school. We'll probably see a lot of the Harrises."

Kenji looked up from the small stack of bills. "Well . . . I'll be damned."

Monday, January 22

T HE WHISTLE BLEW FOR THE shift change and the shipyard workers began to pour out of the shops to make their way home. Isaac Washington joined the stream of men, lunch pails in hand, heading for the dock where they would board the long, low boats that would carry them across the Mare Island Strait to the Ferry Building. From there, at the foot of Georgia Street, he would catch a city transit bus that would take him within a block of home.

Though the crowd of men was mostly white, Isaac's was not the only black face in the throng heading for the dock. Born and raised in rural Alabama, it was still something of a shock to him to be working in a place where there were no back-of-the-bus edicts and no facilities or water fountains labeled "Colored." Oh, there were definite lines, but they were far more subtle in this blue collar, lunch pail, Navy shipbuilding town.

Isaac merged into the queue filing down the gangway to load the ferry. A sign on top of the cabin proclaimed that the little boat had a name: the Heron. He saw that another boat was gliding up to the dock, ready to load as soon as the Heron pulled away. "All aboard," came the call and the boat eased away from the dock. The skipper advanced the throttle to full ahead and Isaac could feel the steady thrum of the engine as they raced across the channel toward the city. Daylight was fading now and he could see the lights of the city glowing in the dusk. All he wanted was to get home and see what Millie had on the stove. Was tonight the night she had promised ham hock and beans? The thought made his mouth water and he realized that he was very hungry.

Isaac had a thing about dinnertime. It was a hard and fast rule that all family members had to be present and accounted for when it was time to sit down at the table. If one of the kids proposed to miss dinner, it had to be for a compelling reason. Casual absences were simply not tolerated. Family time around the dinner table was sacred as far as Isaac Washington was concerned. It was a time to share the events of the day and every family member was expected to participate. Now, with his daughter Bobbie home again after a year away at college, the family unit would be complete: Isaac, Millie, Bobbie and his son Lucas. He relished having everyone under his roof.

The ferry pulled up to the dock, the lines were secured and the men began to stream up the gangway and onto the dock. Buses were waiting in the lot across from the Ferry Building, doors open, motors running. Isaac smiled and nodded to the driver as he boarded and dropped his token in the fare box. He took a window seat near the front of the bus and settled back for the ride home.

He wondered if he had been too strict with his kids as they were growing up—too rigid, too demanding, too many rules? He'd always demanded a certain standard of behavior, especially when they were little. Bad behavior was met with a warning: "Knock it off! Now!" If that command wasn't obeyed, the kids could count on a swift smack on the backside. That usually did the trick. But was it too much? Isaac wondered if he'd do it differently if he had it to do over.

There was no arguing with the results. Bobbie and Lucas had grown up to be fine young people, polite, respectful, and loving. He couldn't be more proud of them: Bobbie, with her keen intelligence and ready wit, not to mention her physical beauty; and Lucas, a junior in high school this year, an outstanding student and a fine athlete. Isaac was sure that he and Millie had done a good job raising their kids.

He was looking forward to a quiet evening with his family. No class to attend tonight, and no need to report for his part-time job. Just a hearty meal, some lively conversation, and a little TV watching, all of it surrounded by the people he loved.

Isaac caught his reflection in the window and realized he was smiling. He could picture Millie, hurrying about the kitchen, the rich aroma of her down-home cooking wafting into every corner of the little house. He couldn't wait to be home.

Out across the Pacific, across the International Dateline, the sun was rising on a soon-to-be historic day: January 23, 1968. In the waters off North Korea, events were unfolding that had no precedent in U.S. history. After a long day of harassment by gunboats and jet fighters of the People's Republic of North Korea, the Navy spy ship USS *Pueblo* had been forced to halt dead in the water. The *Pueblo* carried a crew of eighty-three men; one of them, Fireman Apprentice Duane Hodges, had been killed as the North Koreans repeatedly fired across the ship's bow. The ship was boarded and the crew was forced to sail into the port at Wonsan where they were taken captive.

It was the beginning of eleven months of beatings, torture, starvation, and public humiliation for Captain Lloyd Bucher and the remaining members of his crew. In the years ahead, it would also come to be seen as a major intelligence coup, not only for the North Koreans, but for their Soviet allies as well. It turns out that the *Pueblo* was loaded with top secret documents and cryptographic equipment and there had not been enough time to destroy all of it.

The carrier USS *Enterprise* was on patrol five hundred and ten miles to the south, yet no aircraft were sent to ward off the enemy. No other warships of the Seventh Fleet were in position to respond. By the time President Lyndon Johnson was awakened with the news, it was too late: any military action would have resulted in the death of the crew.

And so a small, slow, virtually unarmed U.S. Navy ship and her crew, operating off the coast of a hostile nation, carrying sensitive documents and equipment, was left completely unprotected to be seized and exploited.

So much for naval intelligence.

Wednesday, January 31

T HE USUAL AFTER-WORK CROWD WAS gathered at Skip's Place for a cold drink and a little conversation, but today was different. Rather than the normal chatter about the Warriors' prospects or what the Giants might do with the coming season, the discussion turned dead serious. All eyes were focused on the television screen as the voice of Walter Cronkite described the events in South Vietnam. The Viet Cong had launched a coordinated series of attacks at more than one hundred locations, including the U.S. embassy in Saigon. The attacks were timed to coincide with the beginning of Tet, the lunar New Year. Now the screen was filled with scenes of battle, with U.S. Marines fighting to push back the attack and secure the embassy grounds. The gang at Skip's watched and listened in shocked disbelief.

"How the hell can that happen? Didn't Westmoreland just say the war was coming to an end?"

"Yeah, something about light at the end of the tunnel?"

"How did they get into Saigon like that? Did they just stroll into town armed to the teeth, and into the embassy, for God's sake?"

"Hell, you listen to all this talk about body counts—sounds like we killed every damn Viet Cong already. Where are these guys coming from?"

"You hear that? They overran Hue. They're actually capturing cities!"

"I don't think Johnson and Westmoreland know what the hell they're doing."

"We should have listened to Curtis LeMay: Bomb 'em back into the Stone Age."

"Oh sure, and bring China into the war on their side, just like we did in Korea."

"I'll tell you the problem: we got our military with one hand tied behind its back. We need to turn 'em loose and let 'em kick ass. They could clean this up in no time."

"Bullshit! We got no business being there. What we ought to do is get our asses out, bring our guys home. The whole damn country isn't worth the life of one American soldier."

"Oh yeah? We pull out of Vietnam and the whole damn region will end up in the hands of the communists. Laos, Cambodia, Thailand, all them countries. All commie! Is that what you want?"

"Oh sure, and look at that fine bunch of individuals we're propping up in Saigon. What a bunch of crooks! They line their damn pockets while our boys do the fighting."

"Well, I'll tell you this: if they draft my kid, I'm sending him to Canada."

"Goddamn, I can't believe you just said that. I thought you were a patriot."

"Hey, don't tell me about patriots. I fought the Japs all across the Pacific and I'm damn lucky to be alive. So don't tell me about patriots!"

The discussion raged on as battle scenes flickered across the screen. Walter Cronkite summed it up: "And that's the way it is, January 31, 1968."

Saturday, February 3

T HE PARTY WAS WELL UNDERWAY when she walked in. John didn't recognize her right away, and he did a quick double-take, as did half the males in the room. There was no mistake: it was Roberta Washington, Bobbie to her friends, Lucas Washington's older sister. John knew she'd been away at school and he hadn't seen her in more than a year. He couldn't believe the changes. She was stunning. She wore a bright multi-colored, loose-fitting top, a pair of fitted jeans, and black knee-high boots. Her hair was grown out into a full afro. Very large gold hoop earrings hung from her lobes and she wore a necklace composed of several strands of white beads. To John, she looked like an African queen, a woman among all the girls at the party.

The house was filled with friends from high school, there to celebrate the birthday of their hostess, a girl named Judy who John had known since grade school. The crowd filled the living room, dining room, and kitchen, kids milling about—talking, laughing, flirting. The family room had been cleared to serve as a dance floor and several couples were rocking out to a Beatles tune playing on the stereo system. Yet in the midst of the hubbub, John could not take his eyes away from Bobbie. Then she looked his way, smiled and waved, and that was all the encouragement John needed. He worked his way through the crowd to get to her.

"Hi, Johnny! How are you?" She gave him a quick hug and a peck on the cheek.

"I'm great, Bobbie. How are you? You look wonderful!" John was never one to be shy, and whatever was running through his mind generally came right out of his mouth.

"You too, Johnny. You've really grown since I saw you last." Bobbie was tall, but she had to look up to John. She judged him to be about six feet three, or thereabouts.

The conversation continued, punctuated frequently by, ". . . what did you say?" due to the the noise level in the house. Finally, John suggested that they step out onto the patio where they could talk without shouting.

The night air was cool and refreshing after the closeness of the house, and they continued their conversation, filling each other in on the events of the past year. John could not believe how she had matured. He remembered her as a cute little girl in the years when they were growing up, attending the same grammar school. Now, she had transitioned from cute through pretty and landed directly on beautiful.

"That's a great blouse, Bobbie. What do you call that style?"

"Thanks. It's a dashiki, kind of an African thing."

"It looks great—with the earrings, the necklace. You look like a queen."

She laughed and changed the subject. "So, how is school going? And what is this now, basketball or baseball season?"

"School is okay, and baseball will start up next week. Lucas and I should see some good playing time this season, even though we're juniors."

"Oh my god, that's right, next year you'll be seniors. The class of '69." She laughed out loud. "I bet you get teased about that."

"Constantly! Let's see, you graduated in '67, right? How's school going for you?"

"Ah . . . not so good. I was at Sac State, but I really didn't know what I wanted to do, plus I ran low on money. So, I'm home again, working, trying to save some money. I'll go back to school when I finally figure out what I want to do." She didn't mention the relationship that had gone bad: a boy who taught her to make love and then dumped her for a graduate student with better long-term prospects.

"Where are you working?"

"I'm working for a janitorial service. We clean some offices and businesses around town. It's good work, and it keeps my days free." She liked the way he maintained eye contact, those pretty blue eyes gazing deep into her own. His blonde hair was a little shaggy and she resisted the temptation to push it back from his forehead with her finger. He'd grown up to be a handsome guy and she was sure there were many young ladies that kept their eye on John Harris.

For his part, John was barely resisting the urge to put his arms around her and hold her close. At last, a pretty ballad came on the stereo system inside.

"Would you like to dance?" He smiled at her and saw her hesitate for just a second.

"Sure," she said. "Why not?"

They stayed on the patio—talking, laughing, dancing when a particular song suited their mood—until the word was passed through the crowd that the party was over and it was time to head for home. John had arranged for his father to pick him up and he knew he'd be waiting outside at the curb. Bobbie was there to take Lucas home. And so they said their goodbyes with another little hug.

"I'll give you a call. Okay?" John didn't hesitate or think twice about it. She was a beautiful girl—a woman, really—and he wanted to see her and talk to her again.

"Bobbie was surprised. Maybe a little shocked. Their eyes locked for a moment, and then she said, "Okay . . . sure . . . call me."

With that, they headed back into the house to thank their hostess.

John Harris, Sr., pulled up in front of the house, killed the engine and turned off the headlights. He rolled down the window and lit a cigarette as he waited. After a few minutes, the front door opened and kids began to stream out of the house, laughing and talking loud, calling goodbye to friends. John Jr. approached the car and opened the passenger-side door.

"Hey, Johnny. How was the party?"

"It was good. We had a good time."

Just then, Bobbie and Lucas Washington passed in front of the vehicle, smiling and waving, heading for Bobbie's car parked across the street.

"What the . . . who the hell is that?" John Sr.'s eyes were focused on Bobbie.

"That's Lucas Washington . . . and his sister Roberta. Remember Bobbie? She graduated in '67."

"What the hell kind of getup is she wearing?"

"It's a dashiki . . . it's an African thing."

"Well, you didn't tell me there'd be coloreds at this party. How many were there?"

"I don't know, maybe six or seven."

"Well, you sure as hell wouldn't have been here if I'd known that."

"Come on, Dad . . . we're friends . . . we all go to school together."

"Goddamn it, Johnny! What's next? First it's parties, then it's dating, then what?"

"Dad, it's not a big deal—"

"The hell it ain't! Look, you don't know these people, son. I do. I grew up with them in Arkansas. They had their own neighborhoods, and their own schools, and their own shops that they did business with, and we got along fine. Hell, some of my best friends were nigras."

"Ah, geez—"

"It's true! And they were happier that way, keeping to their own kind, Johnny. We didn't have the troubles then that you have now."

"Dad, we don't live in Arkansas, and this isn't the good old days—"

"Goddamn it, don't get smart with me! By God, I'm telling you the way it is! Do you hear me?"

"Yes, sir."

It was quiet then. John stubbed out his cigarette and rolled up the window. He started the engine and pulled away from the curb. John Jr. thought about Bobbie, how beautiful and regal she looked dancing with him in the dim light on the patio. He'd give her a call tomorrow.

Bobbie drove across town, heading for home, making small talk with Lucas about the party.

"Lucas, tell me about John Harris. What kind of guy is he?"

"Johnny? Good guy . . . good teammate . . . probably going to get a scholarship, either baseball or football. Why, what's up, sis? Is that who you were hanging out with all night?"

"We talked for a while."

"Oh, my my my! Since when did you develop a taste for blue-eyed blondes?"

"Stop it. We just hung out for a while. He seems nice."

"Well, you'd better watch it, Bobbie. I'm serious. You know how Daddy feels about salt 'n pepper couples . . . about white folks generally."

"Believe me, Daddy has nothing to worry about. John just seems nice, that's all."

They rode along in silence for a while. Bobbie couldn't help but wonder if John Harris would actually call her.

Wednesday, February 21

K ENJI DROVE ACROSS TOWN IN his pickup truck, hurrying to check in with the crews he had working around the city. His first stop would be on La Cresenda in the midst of a beautiful neighborhood on the hill above the high school. His customer, Mrs. Lev, had requested some additional pruning work and he wanted to make sure it was done to her satisfaction. The black script on the side of the truck read "Hashimoto & Son/Landscaping." He had taken the name from his father's business, the business that was lost during the war years. He wondered if his father would be proud of the growth he'd achieved here in Vallejo. He'd never know the answer to that one: his father died shortly after the war, most likely of a broken heart.

The Lev home was a beautiful property, perched on the hill overlooking the high school campus. Ruth Lev was a good customer and Kenji took care to make sure she was happy with his work. It was a little past noon when he pulled up in front of the house. He saw his three-man crew, including his nephew Mark, sitting on the front lawn under a large sycamore tree, taking their lunch break. He spoke to the men briefly and then went to check on the pruning job. Just then, the front door opened and he heard a voice calling to him from inside the house.

"Mr. Hashimoto . . . Mr. Hashimoto . . . could you come here please?"

Kenji approached the front door and saw that Mrs. Lev was standing inside, the screen door securely fastened. "Yes, Mrs. Lev. How are you today?"

"Mr. Hashimoto, if you don't mind, please ask your men not to take their lunch on the front lawn. Please, can you ask them to move? I called to them earlier, but they ignored me."

"Ma'am? Is there something wrong?"

Kenji was a little confused. In his dealings with Mrs. Lev, she'd always been nervous and a little skittish, as though she had reason to be afraid of him and his men. But this was new. She didn't want them to be seen on her front lawn?

"Please ask them to move, Mr. Hashimoto. What will the neighbors think?"

Kenji's temper flared briefly. *Well, they'll think you hired some Japanese lawn jockeys.* He started to respond, then decided it wasn't worth it. He'd ask the guys to finish their lunch in the truck.

"Okay, Mrs. Lev, I'll have them move. Then I'm going to check on the pruning you requested."

He tipped his hat and started to move away from the door. He saw her reach for the latch, making sure it was secured, and then he saw her forearm. She wore a denim shirt with the cuffs rolled up a turn or two, and now, as she reached for the latch, he could see part of the number tattooed on her arm. *Oh, my God!* He almost said it out loud. He knew that Ruth Lev was Jewish, but until that moment, he did not know that she was a Holocaust survivor. He walked away from the door toward where his crew was lounging on the lawn, smoking cigarettes and chatting quietly. He felt for the keys in the pocket of his khaki pants and realized his hand was shaking.

"Okay guys, let's finish your break out in the truck. And don't leave any butts on the lawn." The men gave a collective groan and began to gather their things. "Didn't you hear Mrs. Lev ask you to move?"

"Ah come on, Uncle, we can't even take our break in the shade?" His nephew grinned at him in his usual wise-ass manner.

"Just do what the lady asked, okay?"

"Are you gonna tap dance for her too, Uncle Tom? Oops, I mean Uncle Kenji."

Kenji moved forward quickly and grabbed his nephew by the collar with both hands. He slammed him back against the trunk of the sycamore tree and held him there. This little punk didn't know that his uncle had the knowledge and experience to crush his windpipe if he wanted to. Kenji held him, pinned against the tree, so angry he was unable to speak.

"Geez, Uncle, I was just joking with you." The grin was gone from Mark's face now.

Kenji loosened his grip. "Go on out to the truck." His voice was choked with anger. He turned and marched away toward the backyard to inspect the pruning work.

Kenji sat on the stone bench under the flowering plum tree, gazing out across his rock garden. The garden was a flat, kidney-shaped space, about eighteen feet long and maybe twelve feet wide. Near the center, he had mounded the earth, placed two medium-sized stones, and planted moss and a carefully pruned Bonsai tree. This central structure was shaped to represent the family's home island of Hokkaido. All around it, the sand and small stones were raked to represent the ocean and its ever-shifting currents.

He looked at the garden and wondered if his father would approve. His father was the master and Kenji knew he could never match his skill. Still, he wondered. Hiroshi Hashimoto would never praise his son openly, but perhaps he would have rested here on this bench, lost in meditation, and that would have been praise enough.

He was still upset about the scuffle with his nephew. It wasn't often that he lost control like that. He thought of Mrs. Lev and the number tattooed on her arm. It occurred to him the he had more in common with her than with his own nephew. They were both camp survivors. Their families had been rounded up and hauled away from their homes, their property seized, their citizenship and their humanity denied. Yet he knew that beyond those simple facts, there was no comparison. There were no gas chambers and no ovens at the camp where Kenji's family was held. What Ruth Lev had seen and experienced, and how she had managed to survive, he would never know or fully understand.

Kenji took a long drink from the cold bottle of beer in his hand. He looked at the label with the bright red script that read "Budweiser/King of Beers." He glanced across the back fence toward John Harris's yard. *Why did I tell that cracker that my name is Ken? My name is Kenji, the name my father gave me,* he said to himself. And from now on, he would buy Sapporo, a good Japanese beer.

Monday, February 26

ELLAMAE BROWN SET THE SMALL overnight bag on the porch and carefully locked her front door. Then she closed the screen door, found the right key and locked it as well. *Dear Lord, watch over this house and keep it safe.* It was one of many little prayers she would say to herself during the day, an ongoing conversation with God that didn't require an Amen, because it was never finished.

She wore a brown cloth coat against the February chill, and under that, her standard work clothes: a simple cotton house dress and crepe soled service shoes—practical, comfortable, perfect for the day's work ahead. She unlocked the door to her '63 Chevy Nova sedan, reached in to unlock the back door, and dropped her bag on the back seat. She stepped into the car, her stout body causing the vehicle to dip and rock a little. Ellamae was about five feet six inches tall and she would admit to one hundred and sixty pounds. When she stood before you and fixed you with her steady gaze, the impression she gave was one of innate strength. It was clear that she was a formidable woman: you did not mess with Ellamae Brown.

She turned the ignition key and listened absentmindedly as the engine sprang to life. She flipped the switch for the windshield wiper to clear away the early morning dew, turned on the defroster and felt a rush of cold air sweep by her forehead. She let the engine idle for a minute or two, until the flow of air began to warm. There was no hurry this Monday morning, no need to rush. Finally, she shifted into reverse and backed out of her driveway, out onto

Florida Street, and began the short drive across town to Ruth Lev's home on the hill above the high school.

Ellamae had worked for Ruth Lev for nearly ten years now, starting as her housekeeper, coming twice a week to clean and scrub the large, well-kept home on La Cresenda Street. But she and Ruth hit it off almost immediately, and soon they had developed an odd friendship, odd because they could not have been more different: Ruth, in her late sixties, born in Germany to a small, close-knit Jewish family, a Holocaust survivor, the widow of a successful banker; Ellamae, also in her sixties, born in rural Alabama to a poor black family, the widow of a shipyard worker.

Those were the surface differences. In the course of many conversations over coffee at Ruth's kitchen table, they discovered the myriad things they had in common. As time went on, their bond grew and Ellamae's job began to evolve. Rather than housekeeping two days a week, she would live in on the weekdays, occupying a room of her own on the second floor, preparing meals, cleaning, and generally looking after Ruth. They would shop together, making trips to the market to restock the pantry, or to the stores downtown to replenish Ruth's wardrobe. They were known around town as Ruthie & Ellie: a true partnership; an unbreakable team.

Of course, their ventures out into the community came on Ruth's good days, when her spirit was bright and the sun was shining. Then there were the days when she closed her bedroom door and would not leave her bed, when her blinds were drawn tightly to keep out the sun, when the thought of food turned her stomach. On those days, which could last for a week or more, Ellamae hovered close by, ready to provide whatever Ruth needed, even if it was only a strong shoulder to cry on.

At first, Ellamae didn't understand the dark times. "Holocaust" was just a word, the full meaning still a mystery to her. Through conversations with her pastor, and then trips to the fine old Carnegie Library downtown, she began to study and learn and understand. The articles she read and the photographs she saw overwhelmed her. The meaning of the number tattooed on Ruth's arm and the miracle of her survival became clear.

25

Now Ellamae was caught in traffic streaming toward the high school, moving slowly along Amador Street. She could have chosen an alternate route, but she didn't mind the slowdown. The hustle and bustle of the young people making their way to the campus somehow energized her. She watched the boys and girls crowding the sidewalk, a slow-moving rainbow, all shapes, sizes, and colors, laughing, talking, flirting, so different and far removed from her own childhood experience. *Lord, bless these beautiful children.*

She passed the intersection with Nebraska Street, then veered right onto Camino Real and began the climb up the hill, through the lovely neighborhood above the school campus. She marveled at the contrast between the homes here and those on her block of Florida Street. Soon, she was turning into the driveway of Ruth Lev's home on La Cresenda, continuing along the north side of the house to the detached two-car garage in the rear. Later, she would park her car in the garage and it would sit there through the week until it was time for her to head for home. Wherever they went during the week, they would take Ruth's Oldsmobile 88, the vehicle Ellamae referred to as the Land Yacht. She wasn't sure of the model year, but it was a fine car, well maintained, the dark blue finish polished to a high gloss.

Ellamae took her small bag from the back seat and made her way to the kitchen door at the rear of the house. She climbed the three steps and readied her key to unlock the door. Through the window, she could see Ruth standing in the kitchen, her back to the door, scooping coffee into the percolator. Ellamae paused for a few seconds, watching the thin, frail-looking woman standing at the counter. Ruth was dressed in her usual uniform: khaki slacks, a white turtleneck sweater, and a denim shirt. She stood watching, wondering which Ruth Lev she would find today: the lovely, warm and embracing Ruth, with her bright and irrepressible smile and the twinkling eyes? Or the dark, depressed Ruth, eyes downcast, unable to eat or sleep, barely able to function?

She rapped softly on the window so as not to startle Ruth, and then inserted her key and unlocked the door. Ruth turned her head, glancing over her shoulder, and smiled her brightest smile.

"Ellie!" She finished with the coffeemaker and plugged it into the outlet on the wall behind the counter. "Welcome home, dear. You're just in time for coffee."

Ellamae felt her heart soar. *Dear Lord, bless Ruthie Lev, and let this be a good week.*

Saturday, March 9

T HEY SAT IN THE LOGE seats of the El Rey theater, watching Benjamin Braddock, *The Graduate,* fumble and stumble his way into the arms of Mrs. Robinson. They laughed out loud at Ben's social blunders, rooted like crazy for Ben and Elaine, the star-crossed lovers, and marveled at how skillfully the music of Simon and Garfunkel was woven into the story. Somewhere between the Taft Hotel and Ben's mad dash for Berkeley, John reached over and took Bobbie's hand, their fingers interlocking comfortably. It was one of those sweet little things he did continually that tended to melt her resistance. She squeezed his hand quickly, and then began trying to rebuild her defenses.

This was another in a series of what they'd come to refer to as "un-dates." They would meet inside the lobby of a theater, or just happen to show up at Scotty's Doughnuts at the same time, or meet at the Miracle Bowl to roll a few lines. John didn't like it, didn't understand why they couldn't date openly, but he accepted it because it meant he could be with Bobbie. Bobbie insisted on the un-date scenario, even though she knew they weren't fooling anyone. Anyone, that is, except their parents. She had too much love and respect for her own parents to defy them openly, but it was getting harder and harder to maintain the charade.

After the movie, she knew they would wind up driving to some secluded spot, out of sight from the world, and then the kissing and touching would begin. She hungered for it as much as John did, but she had drawn a hard line beyond which she would not go. She pleaded with him to slow it down, telling him they'd come too far too fast, but then it would start again and the words would come tumbling out of his mouth: "I love you, Bobbie. I love you."

Bobbie wanted to let go, to just let it be, to say "I love you too," but she held on tight, afraid that if she crossed that line, it would be like jumping from a plane without a parachute. When she was alone and he wasn't holding her and kissing her, she could tell herself that it was wrong and stupid. He was a junior in high school, for God's sake! He barely had his driver's license. She was almost two years older. Maybe that was it: she was his Mrs. Robinson. His *black* Mrs. Robinson. The idea made her laugh, and shake her head at the same time.

His simple directness charmed and confused her at first, but she finally figured it out. John had the ability to be completely in the moment, no concerns about the past, no fear of future consequences, totally and completely focused on the here and now. It was part of the reason he was a fine athlete: he could strike out twice, for example, looking ridiculous, then line a shot off the wall in his next at bat. She came to see that it was his greatest strength, and his biggest weakness. Especially where she was concerned. Especially when they were alone together.

They walked out of the theater, talking and laughing over scenes from the movie, heading toward his car in the parking lot. He took her hand again and she didn't resist. Bobbie thought of the closing scene, with Ben and Elaine riding away from the church in the back of the bus, Ben a picture of hope and happiness, and Elaine's beautiful face suddenly stricken with the question: *Oh my God, what have I done?* She knew that except for the color contrast, John was Ben and she was Elaine. It scared her a little and she shuddered involuntarily.

"You okay?"

"Yeah, sure," she said.

She looked up at him then, walking next to her, so strong and sweet and sincere, the muscles in his forearm rippling as he squeezed her hand. God, he was a beautiful boy, his body sculpted by constant training for one sport or another. If there was an ounce of fat anywhere, she couldn't see it—or feel it.

"Let's go someplace where we can be alone," she said. And she tightened her grip on his hand.

Sunday, March 31

A FEW REGULARS SAT ON their favorite stools down at Skip's, chatting and laughing, ignoring the television mounted above the bar where President Lyndon Baines Johnson was delivering an address to the nation.

"Whoa, did you hear that? Listen up guys." Skip reached for the set and turned up the volume.

Suddenly, all eyes were glued to Johnson's image on the screen. They watched the conclusion of the President's remarks, and then watched the pundits and commentators appear on camera, looking like they'd been sound asleep and rudely tossed out of bed, scrambling to seize control of the moment.

"And . . . ah . . . the President said . . . ah . . . do we have that tape? No? . . . ah, well . . . Dan, I believe his exact words were, 'I will not seek, nor will I accept, the nomination of my party for another term as your president.' Do we have that tape now? Okay, let's roll it."

And there on the screen flashed the replay, the image of a tired and beaten man saying in effect that he was stepping aside, that he would not run for re-election, that he was ordering a halt to the bombing of North Vietnam in hopes of bringing all parties to the peace table.

"Well, I'll be damned. Old LBJ is throwing in the towel. Never thought I'd see the day."

"That man's been in the thick of it since the thirties. How's he gonna retire? It'll kill him."

"I'll tell you what's killing him: it's that damn war; a thousand dead American kids coming home in coffins every month. That's what's killing him."

"Well, he took us into it. Wanted to 'nail that coonskin to the wall' and all that shit. Now he's got demonstrators outside the White House chanting 'Hey, hey, LBJ, how many kids did you kill today?'"

"It was that damn McNamara and the brass hat generals. They sold him a bill of goods. 'Give us the men and the bombs and we'll have the boys home by Christmas.' Christmas, my ass!"

"You know that Gulf of Tonkin thing was a phony. Just an excuse to start bombing in the north."

"Now we got five hundred thousand men over there and Walter Cronkite says it's a stalemate."

"It's a sad state of affairs when people trust Cronkite more than the president."

"Well, I tell ya what: Lyndon was a master in the Senate. There was nobody that could get things done the way he could. As president, too. You watch: we'll never see another president work congress the way he did."

"You're right about that. Voting rights. Public accommodations. Medicare. Housing rights. He knew how to get it done."

"And you're *for* all that crap? We give the coloreds—or the blacks, or African-Americans, or whatever they want to be called now—their civil rights and what do they do? They burn down their own neighborhoods! Los Angeles, Newark, Detroit, you name it."

"Hey, look: 'We hold these truths to be self-evident. That all men are created equal.' It's damn well time we lived up to it, and LBJ knew that."

"So you want 'em living next door to you?"

"I think I'd rather have them than you." (laughter)

"Remember when he said 'We can have guns and butter too'? Turns out he had to choose. Turns out you can't have both."

"Yeah, well, you can take all of his Great Society crap and shove it. Who's gonna pay for it? I'll tell ya who: working stiffs like us, that's who. And we'll all go bankrupt together."

"Just wait 'til you sign up for Medicare. You'll appreciate good old LBJ then."

"Who are the Democrats going to nominate now? McCarthy's a one-issue guy. I don't think he's got the stuff."

"Humphrey will jump in. And LBJ will probably endorse him."

"I think Bobby Kennedy is the man to beat. When he announced that he was running, I think Johnson was really hurt."

"Ah, geez, just what we need: a return to Camelot. The damn Kennedys think they're a royal family or something."

"So LBJ's going back to the banks of the Pedernales, back to the ranch. I don't think we'll ever see his like again."

Skip went about counting the money and closing out the cash register. Over his shoulder, he could see Bobbie and Thad, the two kids from the janitorial service, stacking chairs on the tables, preparing to sweep and mop the black and white tile floor. They were both in their late teens and Skip had come to admire their work ethic. They were quick and efficient and they left the whole place—the kitchen, the restrooms, the bar itself—spotless every night. He noticed that they were playful and affectionate, their conversation light and easy and punctuated with laughter, and he wondered if they were a couple. They were nice looking kids, both of them: dark skin, dark brown eyes, trim and athletic looking, and they both wore their hair in the Afro style that was currently in vogue.

Skip remembered the call from the service that afternoon, advising him that Thad would be leaving the company; he had been drafted and would leave for basic training in about a week. The manager assured him that a suitable replacement would be assigned, and that Bobbie would continue on the job.

"Hey, Thad, got a minute?" Skip called the young man over.

"Yes, sir?"

"Your boss called today, said you got drafted, that you'll be leaving us."

"Yeah, I leave a week from Monday." Thad managed a weak smile.

"Well, we're gonna miss you around here. You did a damn fine job."

"Thank you, sir. Bobbie is going to continue on your account. You're a good customer. I'm sure the company will take care of you."

"Thad, if you don't mind my asking, are you and Bobbie a couple?"

"Me and Bobbie? Nah, she's my cousin. We're family."

"Oh. Well, here's wishing you all the best, young man." Skip reached his hand across the bar and Thad shook it firmly.

"Thank you, Mr. Marks." He turned and started to walk away.

"Thad, let me ask you something . . ."

"Yes, sir?"

"Did you see the president's speech tonight? What do you think about that?"

Thad was a little startled. In his experience, middle-aged white men didn't often ask black teenagers for an opinion. "Well . . . I think he led us into this thing. And now it's not going so well. And he's gonna take his marbles and go home. Where does that leave the rest of us?"

Skip thanked Thad again for his hard work and watched him walk away, back to the job of mopping the tile floor. Those words would come back to him in the months ahead: *Where does that leave the rest of us?*

Tuesday, April 2

I SAAC WASHINGTON SHOOK THE LAWN chair open with his left hand and sat down. Under his right arm, he carried the books and notebooks that he intended to study. The ground was uneven and the chair rocked a little as he settled in. He was sitting just outside the center field fence at Wilson Park, his car parked behind him at the curb. He was determined to kill two birds with one stone. He was there to watch his son Lucas play baseball, but he was also coming down to the wire in his exam preparation and he needed the study time as well. He watched Lucas trot out to his position in the outfield and they exchanged nods. It was a sunny, breezy afternoon with a few puffy clouds sailing overhead. The grandstand behind home plate was about half full and in a minute or two, the game would be underway.

He ran down his study outline, cracked one of the books and began to review the underlined passages. The exam to become a registered nurse was just one short week away. He was determined to be ready, even if it meant cramming night and day for the next week. A lot depended on passing this test: a job he'd dreamed of for years; a career he could be proud of; a brighter future for his family. Those were not easy things to come by for a black man. If he failed to pass this exam, it would not be for lack of effort.

It had been a long hard pull to reach this crossroads. The two-year community college program had taken him four years to complete, given the demands of working and supporting a family. And when he passed the test, and by God he would pass it, he'd still have to go out and find a job. Nothing was certain except for the burning ambition that drove him to be something *more*.

Isaac worked as a janitor on the shipyard. It was good honest work and it paid the bills, or most of them anyway. He supplemented his pay by picking up part-time jobs with a couple of janitorial services in town. Yet he longed for the day when he would put his broom and mop aside for the last time. That day was coming.

The game and his studies progressed. He paused when Lucas came to bat and watched his son line a base hit to left field. He was about to return his attention to the book in his lap when he saw Big John Harris heading his way.

John Harris was a notorious pacer. He could not sit still in the grandstand when his son was on the field, especially when he was pitching. John would walk back and forth around the outfield fence, pausing occasionally to light a cigarette, and then moving on in a never-ending fidget.

Isaac saw John heading his way and braced himself for impact. *Just what I need: this big honky comin' out here to mess with me.* Their sons had been teammates through several seasons and he was familiar with John's larger-than-life persona: talking loud with his Southern drawl, as though the world was waiting eagerly to hear his opinion. Isaac looked around quickly, but there was no place to run. Study time was about to come to an end.

"Hey, Ike! What are you doin' out here all by yourself?"

Isaac's friends called him Ike. It irked him to hear it from John Harris. "Hey, Big John. How's it goin'?"

"Say, that son of yours is a fine ballplayer. He can really swing the bat. Junior tells me he's a good student too. A real credit—"

Isaac flinched a little. *Oh, sweet Jesus! Was he going to say 'a credit to his race?' And what race would that be? The human race?* He bit his tongue. "Yeah thanks, John. Lucas has always done well in school."

"So, that's some pile of books you got there. What are you doin'?"

"I'm studying for an exam, the registered nurses exam. I have to take it next week."

"Registered nurse? Well, I'll be damned. I thought all them RNs were women?" John looked at Isaac with suspicion.

"Not all of 'em, Big John. It's something I've wanted to do for a long time."

"Well . . . why in God's name would you want that?"

Isaac closed his book with a thump that was a little too loud. "I was a medic in the Army during the war. I liked helping people. It's just what I want to do."

"The Army you say? Well, I'll be . . . where did you serve?"

"Italy, with the 92nd Infantry Division. The Buffalo Soldiers."

John Harris was stunned. An Army medic. A fellow veteran of World War II. He didn't know what to say.

A young girl came running along the fence, toward where the two men were conversing. It was John's 12 year-old daughter Jenny, all legs and elbows, her blonde ponytail bouncing as she ran.

"Daddy, can I get a hot dog and a Coke? Mom said to get some money from you. Can I?" She grabbed her father's hand, bouncing beside him, smiling up at his craggy face. "Hello, Mr. Washington." She gave Isaac a smile and a little wave.

"Sure, darlin'. Come on, I'll go with you. See ya' later, Ike. Good luck with that exam."

With that, they were gone, back along the outfield fence, heading for the snack bar. Isaac watched them walk away, holding hands and laughing. *So, that old cracker has a soft heart after all. That little blondie is the apple of his eye.*

He opened his book and tried to find where he'd left off.

Thursday, April 4

A COUPLE OF GUYS WALKED into Skip's Place, spied a friend and made their way over to the bar.

"Hey, did you hear about this?" The friend was indicating the television mounted above the bar where Walter Cronkite looked sternly into the camera, the fresh news copy held firmly with both hands. The voice-over introduction concluded and Cronkite began:

"Good evening. Dr. Martin Luther King, the apostle of non-violence in the civil rights movement, has been shot to death in Memphis, Tennessee . . ." He went on, the voice strong and unwavering, the nation's trusted Uncle Walter, come once again to deliver tragic news. The mood at the bar was quiet and solemn as Cronkite finished his report.

"Oh boy, we're in for it now. You watch—the cities will burn again."

"And who's going to step up now? King was already losing control. We're gonna see a lot of guys like Stokely Carmichael and H. Rap Brown."

"What about Eldridge Cleaver and Huey Newton?"

"Well, I think Dr. Martin Lucifer Coon got what he was asking for."

"Hey, watch it. The man's dead. Have a little respect. At least he was for non-violence."

"Yeah, well you know J. Edgar Hoover has a file on King. His organization is full of commies."

"Ah, bullshit. Where do you get this stuff?"

"Everybody knows that! Just wait, it'll come out in the news."

"I say you're full of shit. He helped a lot of people stand up for their rights."

"The man could speak, and write too. Letter from a Birmingham Jail. I have a dream. He had some voice."

"Hey, you can't go down there in the South and tell those folks how to live. They were doin' just fine without a bunch of do-gooders from up north stirring up all the nigras."

"He wasn't from 'up north.' He was from Georgia or Alabama or someplace. And listen to you: 'nigras' isn't even a word. Why don't you go ahead and say 'nigger.' That's what you mean."

Skip moved toward the group at the bar, determined to calm the debate. "Hey, look, let's keep it down a little. I don't want to hear the word 'nigger' in here. Nobody's a nigger. Okay?"

"Well damn, Skip, I never took you for a nigger lover!"

Skip reached under the bar and gripped the Louisville Slugger mounted there on a rack. He wouldn't hesitate to tap this guy if it came to that. "Look . . . see that door over there? Right outside across the strait is the shipyard. I get lots of folks in here, coming from the yard, ship fitters and boilermakers and sailors and marines—white, black, yellow, brown—they all come through that door. If they behave themselves and they've got the price of a drink, they're welcome. And nobody is gonna call 'em names. Not in here. My place, my rules. Got it?"

The man scooped up his change, cursing under his breath, and headed for the door. Skip let go of the bat and moved down the bar to another customer. On the television screen, the photo of King's closest associates, standing on the balcony of the Lorraine Motel and pointing to where the shot was fired, was being seared into the nation's memory.

Skip was finishing up behind the bar, nearly ready to turn out the lights. The front door was locked and the bar was empty, except for Thad and Bobbie who were wrapping up their cleaning duties for the night. Above the bar, the television was tuned to a station out of the Bay Area. The screen displayed a plain white background with the words, "In Memoriam/Dr. Martin Luther King, Jr./January

15, 1929-April 4, 1968." Gospel music played in the background. One song ended, and then the voice of Mahalia Jackson came on, slow and clear and strong, singing "Precious Lord."

> *Precious Lord, take my hand*
> *Lead me on, help me stand*
> *I am tired, I am weary, I am worn . . .*

Skip watched as Bobbie sat down hard on a chair out on the floor, her face in her hands, her body racked with sobs. He saw Thad go to her side and put his arm around her slender shoulders. And now he could hear her sobs, coming in great spasms with every breath. He braced himself against the counter in back of the bar, his chin dropped to his chest. Until that moment, his concerns had been for peace in the cities across the country, for who would step into the void left by King's death, and whether the teachings of non-violence would be lost forever. He had not considered for one minute the wrenching personal loss that would be felt by black people everywhere, especially kids like Thad and Bobbie. He walked around the bar and across the room to where they were holding on to each other.

"Look, Thad, Bobbie, I can finish up here. Please, go on home and be with your families."

They protested but he insisted, and finally, he walked them to the door to let them out. As they went into the cool morning air, their arms wrapped around one another, he called after them: "Thad . . . Bobbie . . . I'm sorry . . ."

He wished there was something more to say, but he knew he'd probably only make it worse.

Friday, April 19

THEY WERE PARKED AT LOVERS' Point in Benicia, looking out at Southampton Bay and the Carquinez Strait. The lights of the C&H sugar refinery and the bridges flickered in the distance. It was another un-date, one of only a few since the King assassination. Bobbie had been withdrawn, conflicted, confused over her feelings for John, not at all certain she should let their relationship continue.

She sat apart from him now, her handbag on the seat between them, listening to him talk about the movie they'd seen that evening. He'd been nothing but supportive since that awful night of April 4, gentle and kind, giving her space when she asked for it, giving her his strong embrace when she needed it. He offered no words of advice or feigned wisdom about a situation he couldn't fully comprehend. His only concern was for her well being, her happiness, her peace of mind. She listened to him, not really hearing his words, lost in her own emotions, and she knew that her feelings for him were growing beyond control.

The movie that evening was a rather strange choice: *Guess Who's Coming to Dinner?* Bobbie knew what the film was about and she really didn't want to see it, but John had convinced her, citing the generally favorable reviews.

"I mean, I think it shows that an interracial couple can make it. Don't you think?" He went on about the story line, pleading the obvious case.

"Sure, if everybody's rich and you live in a mansion, and your dad is Spencer Tracy and your mom is Katharine Hepburn." Bobbie hated to burst his bubble. He was so earnest. "Tell me something: what did you think of the scene where Sidney Poitier is kissing the girl as they drive away in the taxi? A black man kissing a pretty white girl. Tell me the truth: did that bother you?"

"What? No! I mean, they're in love. Why should it matter who's black and who's white?"

"Come on, Johnny. It matters to a lot of folks. There are states in this country where that movie is never going to be seen."

She wanted to add: *A scene like that sends some folks looking for a rope.* She held her tongue, seeing that he was a little hurt and deflated by her resistance to the movie's message. Could he really be so naïve? She felt her heart go out to him. She moved her purse out of the way and slid across the seat to be close to him, her head resting on his shoulder. She turned toward him and kissed him full on the mouth, and she knew from that first kiss there would be no holding back tonight. In a matter of minutes, they had crossed Bobbie's line in the sand and were far beyond where they'd ever been before. Soon her panties were a wet joke on the floor of the car and she heard herself saying, "I love you, Johnny . . . I love you . . . I love you . . ." as they came together.

And then she was out of that proverbial plane, free-falling, the ground rushing up to meet her, and not a parachute in sight.

Thursday, April 25

Ellamae was busy in the kitchen preparing breakfast when the phone rang. She let it ring, waiting for Ruth to answer. Realizing that Ruth was probably still in the shower, she reached for the wall-mounted phone.

"Lev residence. Can I help you?"

"Oh hi, Ellie. It's Skip, Ruth's nephew."

"Skip! How are you, honey? It's good to hear your voice."

They exchanged small talk for a minute or two, and then Skip got straight to the point.

"Ellie, I'm glad you answered so that you can handle this with Aunt Ruth. I had a call from the bartender at Pharaoh's. It's a bar out at the end of Sacramento Street. He tells me that Milton has been out there most of the morning, drinking himself silly, and he refuses to leave. Milt is supposed to be working. The City truck is parked in back of the bar and his work partner is there, trying to reason with him, but he won't listen."

"Lord, have mercy. What's gotten into that boy?"

"Anyway, I'd go out there and get him myself, but I'm alone here at my place and I can't leave. I thought maybe . . . you know . . . maybe he'd listen to you."

"Lord, Lord, Lord! Okay, honey, you let me handle it. I'll see what I can do."

They said their goodbyes and Ellamae put the handset back in its cradle. Ruth would be in for breakfast soon—a soft-boiled egg with wheat toast—and then Ellamae would make an excuse to leave the house to run an errand of some sort. She knew the bar Skip had mentioned by reputation, a broken down dive that ought to be closed for all the trouble that went on there. Would young Milton, Ruth's grandson, listen to her? Could she drag him out of there and send him back to work? Or home to sleep it off? Well, if he knew what was good for him, he'd listen and do what he was told! *Lord, watch over that dear lost child!*

Ellamae drove along Sacramento Street, careful to stay within the speed limit, wondering just what she would find at this bar called Pharaoh's. Milton Lev had been a cause for concern in the Lev family for many years now, in and out of minor scrapes, dropping out of college, and lately moving through life as though hanging out in bars and consuming large quantities of alcohol constituted a career path. Ellamae first met him when he was an adorable nine year-old, full of mischief, always a little gleam in his eye, plotting his next adventure. He would visit Ruth on weekends and holidays and she would shower him with love and attention, and the latest toys that caught his fancy. Of course, when he got out of line, which was often, it fell to Ellamae to administer the appropriate discipline. She would take him by the ear and march him to the corner of the kitchen, sit him down on a little wooden footstool and make him stay there until he apologized for his latest misdeed. In spite of all that, Ellamae loved him almost as much as Ruth. He could be, and often was, the sweetest child in the world.

The family assumed that young Milton would eventually graduate from an acceptable university and join the family business. But Milton had little interest or aptitude for school, and even less interest in banking. Strings were pulled and favors called in to get him admitted to the University of California at Berkeley, but that lasted only until mid-term exams when it became clear that he was failing all of his classes. He left Berkeley and returned to Vallejo, eventually landing a job as a laborer with the City Street Department. And that is how the scion of a prominent and highly respected family came to be wielding a shovel on the streets of Vallejo.

Ellamae pulled into the parking lot in front of Pharaoh's and killed the engine. She glanced at the building, little more than a rundown shack with neon beer signs in the windows. A young man wearing stained denim work clothes was standing near the front door and she assumed it was Milton's partner. She gathered her purse and reached for the door handle. *Lord, give me the strength to carry on.*

"Hi," the young man said tentatively as Ellamae approached the front door. "Are you Ellie? Skip called and said you were on your way."

"And who is asking?" Ellamae fixed him with an icy stare.

"I'm Bill. I work with Milt. We're partners, at least for today."

"All right, Bill. Tell me what happened."

Bill looked away from her withering gaze, feeling a little embarrassed, though he wasn't sure why. "Well, we started out this morning, assigned to fill potholes. We drove up to Basalt and got a couple of yards of hot patch. Milt insisted on driving on the way back. He came here, went inside, parked his ass—excuse me—sat himself down on a barstool and started drinking. He won't leave, and he won't give me the keys to the truck. If he gets caught here drinking, he'll lose his job for sure, and I'll probably lose mine." He paused for a minute. "So, that's it." He shrugged then and waited for Ellamae's response.

She pushed past him and went into the bar, standing near the door while her eyes adjusted to the light. At the left end of the bar were two customers locked in earnest conversation with the bartender. Milton was sitting at the far right end, drinking beer from a long-necked bottle, an empty shot glass in front of him. He did not see Ellamae enter the room. She crossed the floor to the bar and stood at Milt's right elbow. He glanced to his right and was startled to see her standing there.

"Ah geez, Ellie! Goddamn it, what the hell are you doing here?"

"You watch your mouth, Milton Jacob Lev! You do not speak that way to a lady!"

"Yes, ma'am." He said it automatically. Old habits die hard. Then he shook his head and continued. "Who sent you, anyway? Why are you here?"

"That don't matter one bit, young man. The question is what are you doing here, drinking your breakfast, putting your job and that young man Bill's job up for grabs? What's got into you?"

"It's none of your business, Ellie. Just back off and leave me alone." He signaled to the bartender for another round.

The man behind the bar approached, holding a piece of ledger paper in his hand. "Look, Milt, it's time to settle up your tab. You haven't paid on this for about a month, man. I'm cutting you off until you make good on this. Okay?"

Milt started to protest, but Ellamae reached out and snatched the paper from the man's hand. Her eyes widened as she looked at the bottom line number.

"Lord, Milton, you got nothing better to do than spend your all your money in this dump? Mercy me!"

"Hey, you callin' my place a dump?" The man was clearly offended.

"If the shoe fits, Mr. Pharaoh! If the shoe fits!" Ellamae glared at him and watched as he took a step back from the bar.

"Look, just see that the tab gets paid, okay?" He knew she was right. It *was* a dump. He worked hard to keep it that way. His patrons *preferred* it that way. *Well, let this nigger bitch say whatever she wants, as long as the tab gets paid. To hell with 'em.* He rapped his knuckles on the bar, then turned and walked away.

"Now you listen to me, Milton. You say this isn't my business. It is every bit my business. You answer me right now! Why are you doing this?"

Milton Lev was no match for Ellamae Brown, never had been. "Okay, okay . . . I'm gonna be drafted. We have friends on the draft board and they told Dad that since I lost my student deferment, my number is coming up . . . soon."

"And your answer to that is to get drunk and lose your job?"

"I can't be a soldier, Ellie. I can't do it. If they send me to Vietnam, I'm as good as dead. I just can't do it."

"Well, sittin' on this barstool ain't gonna fix anything. You come with me now. You're either going back to work, or home to sleep it off. And that's that."

"And what if I won't go?" Milton found a little bit of courage, though it wasn't much.

"You'll come with me right now, Milton Jacob!" And with that she reached out and grabbed his earlobe between her thumb and forefinger, pulling him relentlessly off the stool.

"Ow, Ellie, for God's sake!" He stumbled off the stool to his right, following her powerful grip, abandoning any thought of resisting. "Okay, okay, just let go of my ear." She released him and a few seconds later, they were out the door and into the bright sunlight.

Bill was incredulous and very grateful. "Oh man, thanks, Ellie. Thanks for getting him out of there."

"What's it gonna be, Milton? Are you going back to work with Just Plain Bill? Or do you want me to take you home?" Ellamae was laying down the law.

Suddenly, Milt took a few quick steps to his left, leaned over to grab his knees and vomited on the side of the building. When he was finally able to stand up, he reached in his pocket and handed the truck keys to Bill.

"Take me home, Ellie. I can't work like this."

"All right, honey. Now, Bill, you tell your bosses that Milton is sick. Something he ate. He'll be okay tomorrow and he'll be back on the job. Got it?"

"Yes, ma'am. And thanks again. See ya, Milt." Bill trotted away toward the back of the building where the large dump truck was parked.

Ellamae realized that she still had the bar tab in her hand. She folded it carefully and put it in the pocket of her coat. She'd discuss it with Ruth when the time was right, sure that the Levs would not want unpaid bills around town bearing their name.

"Come on, child, let me get you home." Ellamae took Milton's arm and directed him toward the little gray Chevy Nova. He went quietly, no need to be led by the ear. *Lord, help this poor lost child. Give him strength . . . and courage.*

Sunday, May 5

JOHN HARRIS STOOD ON THE sidewalk on the north side of N Street, taking in the well-maintained vista of Capitol Park in Sacramento. He took Martha's hand as they started down the broad walkway that led past the east entrance to the Capitol Building. They came to a spot near an ancient magnolia tree and John came to a halt. Across the grass and through the trees, he could see the landscaped grotto that housed the monument.

"There it is, Martha." John gestured toward the structure in the grotto.

"I see it, honey. Are you going to be okay?"

"Yeah. Just give me a few minutes."

He was there at his doctor's suggestion to confront his demons, to see if they could be beaten back, or at least controlled. If he could do this, then maybe the nightmares would subside. Maybe he could even sleep through the night. He continued north along the walk and then turned right onto a paved path named for former governor Hiram Johnson. And then he was standing in front of the monument to the USS *California*.

The *California* was John's ship. He'd joined the crew in January of 1944 when she sailed from Bremerton, Washington. The Puget Sound Navy Yard had repaired the damage sustained at Pearl Harbor on December 7, 1941, and the *California* would go on to fight in battles all across the Pacific, exacting a heavy measure of revenge against the Japanese. Her great 14-inch guns became an important part of the battery that would be arrayed to pound each successive island before the Marines went ashore, firing shells the weight of a small car against the shoreline defenses.

Then came the day, the battle of Lingayen Gulf, when a *kamikaze* came screaming out of the clouds, leveled off and roared into the *California's* superstructure. That was January 6, 1945. Forty-four men died that day; more than one hundred and fifty were wounded. Emergency repairs were made on the spot; ship and crew fought on. More than two weeks later, when the job was done, the *California* steamed back to Puget Sound for permanent repairs. John was reassigned and he finished the war out of harm's way. But the *California* returned to service in the Pacific, first at Okinawa and, finally, supporting occupation forces in Japan.

For John Harris, it was only the beginning. He would relive January 6, 1945, over and over in his dreams. He would see himself frantically feeding ammunition to the anti-aircraft gun, see the *kamikaze* glide into a level path headed for the ship, see the gunner firing desperately at the plane, and watch helplessly as it sailed overhead to explode against the ship. In his dream, he could feel the heat from the fireball, and he could hear his shipmates scream in agony amid the flames.

Now he was standing in front of the monument. It was a simple structure: two square stone columns supporting a stone cap across the top with the inscription: U.S.S. CALIFORNIA. From the crosspiece hung the ship's bell, its clapper removed. The *California* was decommissioned in 1947 and sold for scrap in 1959. This bell was all that remained of a once mighty warship. The carved legend on the left column read:

ONLY BATTLESHIP BUILT ON THE PACIFIC COAST
LAUNCHED AT MARE ISLAND NAVY YARD NOV. 20, 1919
SHIPS BELL DEDICATED AND RUNG FOR THE LAST TIME
BY EARL WARREN OCT. 27, 1947.

On the right column, the World War II battles were listed in order: Pearl Harbor, Marianas, Leyte Gulf, Surigao, Lingayen Gulf, Okinawa, Japan.

John read the inscription on both columns, and then read it again. When he got to the line that read RUNG FOR THE LAST TIME, he felt his blood begin to boil. *Rung for the last time . . . It should be rung every year on November 20, the day she was launched at Mare Island. Rung for the last time . . . It should be rung every December 7, once for each man who died at Pearl. Rung for the last time . . . It should be rung every January 6, for the men who died in the flames at Lingayen Gulf.* His chest was heaving now, his breath coming in great gasps. *Sold for scrap in 1959. Sold for scrap? How do you sell steel for scrap when it has been washed in the blood of brave men? She should be afloat today, with a special berth at Mare Island, open to the public. Let people stand under those guns and imagine the roar and how they lit up the night sky. Let them stand on the spot where the bomb penetrated her hull at Pearl. Let them touch the scorched and twisted steel plate where the kamikaze hit. Let them see, and touch . . . and maybe even feel.*

His breathing was returning to normal now. He removed a handkerchief from his back pocket to mop his forehead and dab his eyes. He felt Martha touch his elbow gently.

"John . . . are you okay, honey?"

"Yeah. I'm fine. I'm fine now." He took two steps forward and placed the palm of his right hand against the surface of the bell. Finally, he stepped away. "Okay, Martha. Let's go."

She wrapped her right arm around his ample waist as they walked away, heading back to N Street and the entrance to the park.

Friday, May 10

"**I** DON'T GET IT. WHAT exactly do they want?"

The regulars down at Skip's looked up at the television, bearing witness to the rioting in the streets of Paris. After a week of protests all across the country, ten thousand students had marched through the streets and straight into a cordon of helmeted riot police. Tear gas hung in the air, concussion grenades were fired, and the police laid into anyone within reach with their hard rubber truncheons. The injured included one hundred and thirty policemen and more than four hundred and forty civilians.

"I think what they want is to get rid of old General de Gaulle."

"Yeah, but he's their great war hero."

"Ah hell, he thinks he *is* France. It's time for him to let go."

"Remember what Churchill called him? 'The Cross of Lorraine.'"

"Well, he was something during the war. And after, too, when he cleaned out all those Vichy collaborators."

"I hear that all the labor unions are going out on strike. They're gonna shut down the whole country."

"Well, the General is gonna have to do something."

"Yeah, like declare martial law."

"I still don't get it. What the hell do they want?"

"It's just like all those kids at Columbia University in New York City. Columbia, for God's sake! Bunch of spoiled rich kids, occupying buildings, tearing down their daddies' institution."

"Hey, it's more than that. They've got something to say, and we're gonna have to listen, whether we like it or not."

"Well, I still don't know what the hell they want."

They sipped their beer and watched the French students heaving stones in the direction of the police. They could tell from the awkward throwing motions that baseball was not the national pastime of France. But apparently the students' aim was good: ten months later, Charles de Gaulle stepped down.

Saturday, May 18

T HEY CUDDLED TOGETHER SPOON-FASHION ON John's bed, his right arm around her, the fingers of his right hand interlocked with hers. Bobbie's eyes were closed, her face a picture of contentment. Was she sleeping? John lifted his head a little, propped up by his left arm, so that he could look at her in the mirrored doors of the closet. His eyes scanned her long, lean, naked body from the top of her head to her feet, tangled in the rumpled bedding. She was wearing a gold necklace that fit closely around her neck, a matching gold bracelet and earrings. The contrast of the bright gold jewelry against her black skin was striking, and again John conjured up the image of Bobbie as a queen, the beloved monarch of some powerful nation. He continued to gaze at her image in the mirror and he felt a stirring in his loins. She felt it too and her eyes blinked open.

"Good Lord, Johnny, don't you ever get enough?" She met his gaze in the mirror and smiled at him.

"No. Never. Not ever enough."

"Oh my . . . you horny little devil." She laughed and pressed her backside against him. "Are you sure your family is gone for the day? Wouldn't be good if they walked in on this scene."

"Yeah, they're gone for the whole day. We have the house to ourselves." He paused a moment, then continued: "Look at you. God, you are beautiful. I can't believe you. You're too beautiful to be real."

She was quiet for a moment, studying their image in the mirror. Then slowly her face began to change, her lips trembled slightly, and tears began to fall from the corners of her eyes.

"God, Johnny, look at us. Who are we kidding? How can we do this? We can't make this work—"

"Shhh . . . it's okay . . . sure we can make it work. We love each other."

"Your family can never accept us. Your father would kill you if he knew. My father would kill me—"

"That's not true . . . my folks will love you when they get to know you."

"Are you serious? Your daddy? From Junction City, Arkansas? My God, Johnny—"

"Shhh . . . it's okay."

"You know this could get me lynched . . . in several states . . . and get you tarred and feathered—"

"We don't live there . . . we're here, and I love you . . . we're okay."

"I love you too. I really do. But there isn't a place in this world where we are okay."

"Don't cry . . . we're here now and there's nobody but the two of us."

She looked in the mirror, struck again by the contrast in black and white, and then she couldn't look any longer. She turned slightly in his arms, then turned again to face him, her head buried against his chest.

"Hold me, Johnny . . . just hold me, and kiss me. Kiss me about a thousand times."

She tried her best to be like him, to live completely in this moment, no history to worry about, no consequences to fear, just this instant in time. He did as she asked and kissed her a thousand times, in places she'd never been kissed before, and they made the moment last for one unforgettable day.

Tuesday, May 28

"**D**ID YOU HEAR ABOUT THE *Scorpion*?"

Skip had heard the question so many times during the day that he'd lost count and could not remember the first person who had asked. The news had spread out across the country in successive shock waves from the epicenter, the Norfolk Navy Base at Hampton Roads, Virginia. It began with a news bulletin broadcast by the CBS television affiliate in Norfolk on May 27 at around 6:00 PM local time: the USS *Scorpion* was overdue in port and the Navy had declared a SubMiss (submarine missing) alert. The crew of ninety-nine officers and enlisted men were drawn from thirty-three of the fifty states and long distance phone lines lit up as families reached out to notify their loved ones.

The second wave came on Tuesday morning, May 28, when major Newspapers across the country reported the SubMiss alert and the fact that the Navy had launched a massive open-water search operation. In Norfolk, *The Ledger-Star* proclaimed, "No Trace of Sub Found as Navy Presses Search." The headline in the New York Times read, "U.S. Nuclear Submarine with 99 Overdue." Again, phone lines were jammed, reaching into every corner of the country, including Vallejo, California.

Vallejo, the home of Mare Island Naval Shipyard, was an integral part of the nuclear navy. Beginning with the USS *Sargo* in 1957 and extending to the USS *Drum* in 1970, Mare Island would contribute seventeen ships to the nuclear submarine fleet, including seven "boomers" (the Navy's nickname for ships armed with ballistic missiles) and ten fast attack boats. Mare Island was also one of several sites for the Navy's nuclear power school. Any tremor that affected a nuclear submarine would be felt in Vallejo.

With the five o'clock shift change on the shipyard, the crowd at Skip's Place began to grow, larger than normal for a Tuesday evening. It seemed that the shipyard workers needed to come together, to talk about what they'd heard, and hopefully, hear some encouraging news about the fate of the *Scorpion*. Skip knew it was just a matter of time until someone would walk in with a story of connections to the ship and its crew. He didn't have long to wait.

"Hey, Robbie. How's it goin'?"

"Goin' good. What's up?"

"Did you hear about the *Scorpion*?"

"What about the *Scorpion*?"

"She's missing. The Navy put out a SubMiss alert yesterday afternoon."

"Damn! That's my brother-in-law's ship!"

All along the bar, eyes turned in Robbie's direction. No one said a word. After several seconds, Robbie broke the silence. "Hey, Skip, I gotta call my sister in Norfolk—"

"Sure, Robbie." Skip didn't wait for him to finish. "Use the phone in the office."

"Thanks, Skip." Robbie hurried toward the door to the small office located off the end of the bar. "I'll pay you for the call."

"Can you believe that? His brother-in-law's ship?"

"Anybody know what class it is?"

"Yeah, it's a *Skipjack*. Built in Groton."

"Did we build any *Skipjacks*?"

"Just one: the *Scamp*. Launched in 1960. It's a good design—faster than hell. I hear it maneuvers like a sports car."

"Yeah, a hundred guys crammed into a sports car. I tell you what: it's no job for sissies."

"You been on one, Jack?"

"Yeah. My last six years were in the submarine service . . . the last three on the USS *Haddo*. She's *Thresher* class."

Now all eyes turned to Jack with the respect due someone who knows.

"Yeah, no job for sissies. You have no idea what it's like out there, underwater for weeks at a time, bored out of your skull, and then all of a sudden you're in places you're not supposed to be, under a Soviet destroyer or some other damn ship, and your heart's pounding so hard you'd swear they could hear it on their sonar. I pissed myself more than once, and that's no lie. Collisions and near-collisions, stuff you'll never hear about, 'cause the Navy doesn't want you to know."

Jack finished his beer and signaled to Skip for another.

"And you have no idea what it does to the wives, either. Killed my marriage, that's for sure. She just couldn't take it—the separations, the silence, the missions you couldn't talk about. She was a good woman, too."

Everyone felt bad for Jack. It was quiet again along the bar. He continued.

"You know, when you're scheduled to go on patrol, they put it to you straight. Make sure your affairs are in order. Make sure your insurance premiums are paid up. Like I said, no job for sissies."

Robbie emerged from the office and rejoined his friends. Skip slid a shot and beer in front of him and he threw back the shot.

"I can't friggin' believe it! My sister says she and the kids were down at the pier in Norfolk, waiting for the ship to come in. They got there at noon and she's due in at 1:00 PM. There's a Nor'easter blowing, the rain practically going sideways. They're waiting in the car, trying to keep warm, stepping out every now and then to see if the ship's coming. One o'clock comes and goes and they're still waiting. Around 4:00, someone from Squadron comes down and tells them she's been delayed and they should all go home. It's easy to believe a delay, 'cause of the lousy weather, so they go home. And on the six o'clock news, they break in with a report that the USS *Scorpion* is overdue and a sub missing alert has been issued. My eight year-old nephew hears this and runs into the kitchen to tell his mom. Can you believe that shit? No call from Squadron. They hear about it on TV."

Robbie was quiet then. His friends bought him another round.

Jack, the former submariner, spoke up. "Hell, as my old man used to say, 'There's the right way, the wrong way, and the Navy way.' I guess this is the Navy way."

"Look, Robbie . . ." Skip felt the need to offer some hope. "Missing doesn't mean lost. She may be out there in the storm somewhere, disabled, unable to radio in. They're launching a search. They could find her . . . anytime now."

"Yeah? Maybe you're right, Skip." He dropped his eyes and thought about it for a few seconds. "I'll have to take some time off . . . check on flights to Norfolk . . . my sister's gonna need some help."

Robbie's friends took his car keys and ordered another round for him. They'd see to it that he got home safely.

In the days and weeks to come, the news would trickle out to the *Scorpion* families and the world at large. Around mid-day on May 27, Memorial Day, the Submarine Squadron 6 command became concerned and began a series of radio transmissions asking *Scorpion* to check in. Receiving no reply, Squadron transmitted alarm up the chain of command, and at 2:15 PM, COMSUBLANT (Commander, Atlantic Submarine Force) requested two reconnaissance aircraft to begin a search along the ship's intended track. Finally, at 3:15 PM, the official SubMiss alert was broadcast to the Atlantic Fleet.

Years later, additional facts would become public knowledge. The last radio transmission from *Scorpion* was received shortly after midnight on May 22, when the skipper, Commander Francis Slattery, gave his current position and said he planned to be in port at 1:00 PM on May 27. Later that day, SOSUS, the then-secret underwater acoustic monitoring system, recorded the explosion that sent *Scorpion* to the ocean floor under eleven thousand feet of water, four hundred miles southwest of the Azores. On May 23, Vice Admiral Arnold Schade, commander of the Atlantic Submarine Force, requested and received approval to launch a top secret search for the wreckage of the submarine.

Of course, the *Scorpion* families, waiting on Pier 22 in the middle of a howling storm on May 27, knew none of this. Not that it would have provided any comfort to know that their sailors were on eternal patrol.

Sunday, June 2

K ENJI FINISHED PRUNING THE BONSAI tree and tending to the moss. He stepped back and admired his work for a moment, put the tools in his pocket and picked up the old wooden rake. He would use it to cover his tracks as he exited the rock garden, rearranging and recreating the flowing pattern in the sand and the stones. He thought about taking a break, resting for a few minutes on the stone bench at the edge of the garden. Then he looked up to see his neighbor, John Harris, approaching the back fence.

"Hey, neighbor. How ya doin'?"

"Hi, John." Kenji could see no way to politely avoid this meeting, so he walked over to the fence.

"I gotta tell ya, Ken, that garden sure is pretty."

"Call me Kenji. Thank you, John. My father always kept a rock garden. I guess I do it for him."

"Well, it's real nice." John could see no earthly value in wasting a piece of ground that could yield vegetables. He was just being polite for a change. "Say, Ken . . . Kenji . . ." He caught himself and went on. "I noticed that your boy didn't play for the Legion team the other day. Saw him on the bench, but not in uniform. He's a fine catcher. Isn't he going to play this summer?"

"Yeah well, we lost his birth certificate in the move and we've got to get an official copy before they can put him on the roster. It's probably going to take a week or so to get it."

"That long? I thought you people were from San Jose or Santa Clara, someplace down there in the Bay Area. Shouldn't take *that* long." John was puzzled. If it was his kid, he'd just drive down there and get it done.

Kenji bristled at the term *you people*, but he let it pass. "It has to come from Arkansas. Rohwer, Arkansas. It's going to take a while."

"Arkansas? Well . . . that's my home state. I was born and raised near Junction City." John paused to mull it over for a few seconds. "So, Eric was born in Rohwer, Arkansas? I thought you were from the Bay Area? What were you doing back there?" Japs in Arkansas! It was beyond John's comprehension.

Kenji wasn't sure he wanted to continue this conversation. *Ah, what the hell,* he said to himself. "My family lived in Santa Clara before the war. We were sent to an internment camp in Arkansas. That's where Tami and I met and were married. Eric was born in Rohwer after the war, before we moved back to California."

John looked stunned. He'd heard about the internment camps, but he'd never stood face to face with someone who had been sent to one, and in Arkansas to boot. Kenji heard the big man say, "Well . . . I'll be damned."

Now Kenji was amused. He had to stifle a laugh that was trying to break out. "John, come on over, let me show you something." Big John did a neat scissor kick over the low picket fence. Kenji led him to the stone bench in front of the rock garden. "Sit right there for a minute. I'll be right back." He hurried into the house and returned shortly with two tall cans of Sapporo. He sat down next to John and handed him one of the cans of beer. "There you go. Now, John . . . have you ever meditated?"

John Harris looked at the can of Japanese beer in his hand, glanced at Kenji sitting next to him, and then looked out across the rock garden. The expression on his face said it all: he had landed on a planet in a strange galaxy, a million miles from home.

"I saw you talking to John Harris today. That was nice." Tami was busy in the kitchen as usual.

"Yeah . . . I was teaching him to meditate." Kenji laughed out loud. "Actually, he was asking why Eric wasn't in uniform for the Legion game the other day. I explained about the birth certificate."

"Oh? What did he say about that?"

Kenji looked up and contemplated the question. "I'd say he was a little . . . surprised, maybe shocked. I don't think he ever considered the possibility of *our people* living in Arkansas. You know, that's where he's from. I was gonna tell him that we are probably cousins, but I don't think he was ready for it."

"Oh, stop it! He's not that bad. And Martha has been very nice since we moved in."

"Yeah, well, maybe you're right. At least he's not marching outside with torches and pitchforks. I guess he's not so bad for a curly-haired round-eye."

Tami gave him an exasperated look, the one that always made him laugh, and went on about her business. "Did you tell him the rest?"

"No. No I didn't."

Kenji knew what she meant. Did he tell John how his family had been uprooted from Santa Clara? How his father insisted all along that he was an American citizen and citizens had rights to due process? How their home had been lost to foreclosure while they were interned in Arkansas? How his father's business had been ruined, his heart broken, unable to start again after the war? No, Kenji had kept that to himself, a conversation for another day. Perhaps Big John would ask one day about the logo on the side of Kenji's truck: "Hashimoto & Son." Then he would tell him the rest of the story.

Tuesday, June 4

I T WAS JUST BEFORE MIDNIGHT and Skip's Place was busy, a good crowd for a Tuesday night. Marty was behind the bar, helping Skip keep pace with the orders. She had a definite bounce in her step tonight. It was primary election night in California and her candidate had been declared the winner by all three networks. She listened casually to the chatter at the bar, refusing to be drawn into any of the debates. She and Skip had an unwritten rule: never discuss politics or religion with the customers; it was bad for business. They did not need to know that she had worked tirelessly for the campaign, making phone calls, stuffing envelopes, walking the precincts and leaving door-hangers on every knob. It was hard not to respond to some of the comments, but she bit her lip and moved on. *He won! We won! There's hope!* She said it over and over as she worked the bar; it was all that really mattered.

And now, just after midnight, all eyes at the bar focused on the television screen, the scene from the Ambassador Hotel in Los Angeles, where Robert F. Kennedy was about to make his victory speech. It was short and to the point: praise for staff and special friends, punctuated with humor, acknowledging that this was just one battle in the war with many more to come.

Marty watched all of this with pride, her smile barely suppressed, wishing that she could just have a few minutes with the Senator from New York to take a pair of scissors to that unruly shock of hair, trimming it just enough to keep it out of his eyes. She wondered how many women were out there, watching this scene, thinking the same thing.

And now his entourage was turning, leaving the podium, heading off the back through a service kitchen. Look—there goes Rafer Johnson, and big Rosie Greer, and Jesse "Big Daddy" Unruh, and of course, Bobby's wife Ethel. Marty turned back to the bar where several patrons were signaling for refills.

And then suddenly the screen was filled with chaos. Shots had been fired. Reporters were shouting into live microphones. The crowd at the Ambassador that had been cheering and laughing just moments ago was gasping, screaming, on the verge of panic. *How many shots? Six? Eight? Get him! Grab him! Get the gun! Break his arm if you have to! Grab him! I want him alive! We don't want another Oswald! The Senator is down! He's been hit! He's been hit in the head! Get back! Get back! Give him air! Is there a doctor here? A doctor, quickly!* A jacket tucked under his head. A rosary placed in his hands . . . *Is there a priest here? We need a priest . . .*

Marty shut the door to the small office that was situated just off the end of the bar. She leaned back against the desk, her arms wrapped around her body, doing her best to stop the shaking. She felt the hot, bitter tears rolling down her cheeks and she looked around the desk and found a box of tissues.

Never again. Never ever again. I'll never let myself get sucked into it again. First with Jack Kennedy, and now with Bobby. You let yourself care, you let yourself hope, you let yourself believe, and then some idiot out there sits in front of his goddamn TV screen and says, "Oh, I could be famous. I could be somebody! Where did I put my gun?" Well, they can all go straight to hell, and they can do it without me. Never ever again. Making the phone calls. Walking door to door. "Can we count on your vote for Senator Kennedy?" Doors slammed in your face. Dogs barking, baring their fangs. And for what? To be a part of this great democratic process, the magnificent, peaceful transfer of power? Peaceful, my ass! Democracy, my ass! It's democracy from a gun barrel. Well, fuck 'em all, unto the hundredth generation. They can all go fuck themselves. Why? Why did I let myself care? Why did I let myself believe?

Skip stuck his head in the door. "Hey, are you okay?"

Marty glared at him, fire in her eyes. Hell no, she wasn't *okay*. She wasn't even on the same planet as *okay*. But . . . he was a good man, her Skip, a damn good man. It wasn't his fault. No need to take it out on him.

She smiled at him weakly. "I'll be okay. What's the latest?"

"He was shot in the head, at close range. They've taken him to a hospital. As far as anyone knows, he's still alive. The guy that shot him—I think they said he's from Jordan—his name is Sirhan Sirhan. That's about all." Skip walked over to where Marty was leaning against the desk.

"Okay. Gimme a minute and I'll be out to help you."

"No hurry, babe. The place is emptying out. Take all the time you need." Skip wrapped her in his arms and they held each other for a moment. "I'm sorry," he said. He kissed her forehead and then turned and headed back to the bar.

Marty's thoughts were tumbling now, looking for a place to land. *Alive? He's still alive? There's hope. I should be hopeful. I should . . . pray.* She closed her eyes and tried to pray for Bobby Kennedy's life, but she couldn't make herself believe. Instead, she prayed for his family—another son, brother, husband, father taken too soon. And she prayed for his mortal soul.

Skip called goodnight to the last group of customers as they headed out the door. The janitors were already busy with the restrooms and it was time to begin closing out the cash register. He was surprised to look up and see a lone customer sitting at the corner of the bar. It was one of his regulars, Ben . . . something. He couldn't remember his last name. He knew Ben was a civilian administrator of some sort at the nuclear power school at Mare Island.

"Ben, what's up buddy? We're closing up now. Time to head for the barn."

Ben raised his glass and gave Skip a shaky salute. Skip was immediately concerned. *Oh man, how many drinks has he had? I served him. I guess Marty did too. I lost count. God, look at him. He's blitzed!*

"Mr. Marks, my good friend . . ." Ben was speaking very slowly, deliberately, trying not to slur his words. "I would appreciate it if you would call a cab for me. I do not wish to drive home in this condition."

"Sure, Ben, happy to do it." He was glad the man's good sense wasn't totally impaired. He placed a quick call to the cab dispatcher.

Ben continued: "I shall be away indefinitely, Skip. Heading east tomorrow. Norfolk, Virginia. I trust you'll hold down the fort in my absence?"

"You bet. What's up, Ben? A new assignment?"

"Temporary duty of indefinite duration. I shall serve on the staff of the court of inquiry on the loss of the USS *Scorpion*."

"Oh yeah?"

"Oh yeah, indeed. You'll see it in the news shortly: the Chief of Naval Operations, Admiral Moorer, will announce that the *Scorpion* is presumed lost. He has already convened a court of inquiry to determine the cause."

"What do you think happened, Ben?"

"That, my friend, is what we need to determine. I shall say no more." With that, he made a zipping motion across his lips.

The front door swung open and a man stepped part way inside. "Cab?" he said with a tired voice. Skip came around the bar and helped Ben off the stool, then toward the door held open by the driver.

"You know, Skip, two of the crew attended nuclear power training here at Mare Island. I looked it up. Christiansen and Huber."

"Geez, Ben, did you know them?"

"No, they were before my time. But their records show they were good men. They were all good men. Ninety-nine good men." Ben's voice was choked with emotion now.

Skip helped him into the cab, closed the door and watched it drive away.

"Damn!" he said. "What a night."

Friday, June 14

T HE COFFEEMAKER PERKED RAPIDLY ON the counter and Ellamae could tell from the aroma that it was nearly done. She placed the pretty serving bowls on the silver tray, filled with tuna salad, egg salad, sliced onions and tomatoes. She added the matching plate stacked high with dark rye bread. Coffee and fresh-baked shortbread cookies would follow the luncheon spread. Ruth's stepson Bradley was home for lunch and Ellamae would serve them at the dining room table. She slid the pocket door open and carried the tray into the room.

"Oh, Ellie, that looks lovely. Bradley, come and sit down." Ruth was always happy to have Brad come to call, but she seemed to be in a somber mood today.

"Ellie, I think you've outdone yourself." Brad smiled at her and took a seat at the table.

Ellamae laughed off the compliments. "I'll be in the kitchen if you need anything." She hurried back to prepare the coffee and cookies. As she worked in the kitchen, she could not help but hear their conversation through the open door.

"We tried our best to get Milton into a Navy Reserve unit, to keep him stateside for the duration of the war."

"And?"

"We weren't able to pull it off. We just don't know the right people there." Brad sounded disappointed, almost apologetic.

"So, he's lost his student deferment, and we can't get him into the Reserve. What other options do we have? I will not see my grandson, even if he's not my blood, in this terrible war, Bradley.

Our family has lost more than its share to war. I will not see it happen again."

"I know, Mom. Here's what we can do. We have friends in Canada. They have a country place a couple of hours outside of Toronto. Milton can live on the estate. I understand there is a carriage house of some sort. He'll be part of the staff that maintains the place—grounds keeping in the warm months, and whatever is needed the rest of the year. We'll see that he receives a stipend. It's good, honest work and he can stay there until . . . well, until it's over."

"And how long is that likely to be?"

"There's no way to know, but I don't think it will be long, now that LBJ has decided to step aside."

Ellamae listened as the discussion continued, torn between closing the door and her amazement at the plans that were being made.

"We're making all the arrangements now," Brad continued. "He'll fly to Toronto, our friends will meet him there. No passport required. He'll have to go through customs, but that's no problem."

"And when will we see him again?" Ruth's voice was shaking now.

"I don't know, Mom. We'll just have to wait and see what happens."

"In the meantime, he'll be safe?"

"Yes, as long as he doesn't go into Toronto or some other town and get into trouble, get himself arrested or something."

"Make sure he understands the consequences."

"I have, Mom, but with Milton, you never know—"

Brad stopped speaking as Ellamae brought the coffee and cookies into the room and placed them on the table. Neither he nor Ruth looked up, their eyes downcast, their expressions grim. It did not happen often, but Ellamae hesitated, unsure of her silent prayer. *Lord, give these folks . . . wisdom . . . and peace.*

She sat in the kitchen of the little wood frame house on Florida Street, her purse resting in her lap. Ellamae had been home for several minutes now, but made it only as far as her kitchen table. Her work for Ruth Lev was finished for the week. She had prepared meals, wrapped and stored in the refrigerator, so that all Ruth would have to do is pop them in the oven. She knew that come Monday, she'd find most of that food untouched. But that was Ruth: not one to sit down and eat when she was alone. Hopefully, Bradley or her nephew Skip would stop by to spend some time with her, get her out of the house for a few hours, perhaps take her to services on Saturday morning.

Ellamae could not pull her thoughts away from the conversation she'd overheard that afternoon. So, young Milton Lev would avoid the war by going to Canada. And this was after other options had been explored and set aside.

She understood Ruth's feelings, having seen her family nearly wiped from the face of the earth during World War II. But what about Ellamae's grandson, Thaddeus Brown, drafted into the Army, finished now with basic training, waiting for deployment? What were his options? Where was his trip to Canada? She had wanted run into the dining room and ask if Thad could accompany Milton. He was a hard worker and he would be a fine addition to the staff on that country place. But she knew it was too late.

Dear Lord, what about Thaddeus? What about my Thad? Ellamae watched as the sunlight faded and dusk began to gather, a lovely orange sunset lighting the sky to the west. She did not move from the kitchen table. Perhaps if she kept perfectly still, God would provide an answer.

Thursday, July 4

J OHN MADE HIS WAY ACROSS the lawn, weaving through the crowd gathered at Waterfront Park. He carried a blanket, two folding beach chairs, and a small cooler containing a variety of soft drinks. He was looking for the perfect spot to spread the blanket, park the chairs and wait for the fireworks to begin. Bobbie would be meeting him near the bandstand; she was working that evening, but had a two-hour break between clients, enough time to enjoy the finale to the Fourth of July celebration.

There was a good crowd gathering, anticipating the fireworks show. The celebration had gone on most of the day, beginning with a parade through town that included bands, a mounted posse, floats with lots of pretty girls, and the usual cadre of politicians and dignitaries. A parade of boats, red white and blue lights strung from the rigging, was making its way up the Mare Island Strait, heading for the Vallejo Yacht Club. On a barge anchored out in the strait, the fireworks technicians were making their final preparations. The clock was ticking down to 9:30 PM, the time promised for the start of the show, and parents all through the crowd were pleading with their children to be patient for just a few more minutes.

John found an open patch of grass, dropped the chairs and the cooler and spread the blanket neatly. He began to scan the crowd, looking for Bobbie. He didn't want her to miss the start of the show. Then he saw her through the crowd, making her way toward him. She was wearing her work clothes, the dark gray pants and lighter gray shirt with the patch on the left breast that read "Aaron's Janitorial." John smiled at her, amazed at the way she made ordinary work clothes look regal. He took her hand as she approached.

"Hi, babe. Come on over here. I've got a good spot." He was happy to see her, as always, and didn't notice that she did not return his smile. He didn't see the concern etched in her face. John opened the beach chairs and they sat down. "Want a Coke?" he asked, indicating the little cooler. She accepted and took a sip of the ice cold drink just as the first volley of fireworks went off.

Suddenly, the sky above them was exploding with successive bursts of white light. The crowd let out a collective gasp, followed by a rousing cheer. This pattern continued with each round launched from the barge, the brilliant display in reds and blues and whites blending in the night sky.

Bobbie was looking at John, watching his smiling face, seeing the colors reflected in his eyes.

"Johnny," she said, leaning close to his ear, "I'm late."

"What? No, you weren't late. I was only here a few minutes—"

"No, Johnny, I mean I'm late."

"What? I don't know—"

A great splash of color filled the sky and the crowd erupted again.

"I mean I'm late." She said it louder this time. "I missed my period."

Another starburst exploded, followed by another cheer, but they were no longer watching. Realization was dawning across John's face, and Bobbie watched closely for his reaction. He smiled and then looked away, back toward the canvas being painted above them, and as he did this, he took her hand in his and squeezed it gently. Bobbie felt the tears welling in her eyes.

They watched in silence until, nearly an hour later, the grand finale lit the sky, bringing the loudest response yet from the crowd. Then they gathered their things and headed out of the park. As throngs of people hurried by, they stood together next to Bobbie's car, talking quietly, trying to sort out their situation.

"Geez, I wonder how this happened? I mean, we tried to be so careful, using rubbers all the time—"

She corrected him: "Most of the time."

"So, what do we do now?"

"Nothing's certain yet. I mean, I haven't been to a doctor or anything."

"Maybe you should go . . . maybe *we* should go."

"Yeah . . . I'll make an appointment . . . soon. But I've got to go to work now. Call me tomorrow, okay?"

She kissed him quickly on the lips and started to pull away, but John held her hands and pulled her close, wrapping her in his arms, her head against his chest. They stood that way for a minute, people streaming past on the sidewalk, shooting disapproving glances in their direction.

"I love you," he said. "We'll get through this. We'll be okay."

Bobbie pulled away and fumbled with her keys, trying to unlock the car door, her eyes clouded with tears. "I love you too, Johnny." She started to add *but it's not enough*, then bit her tongue.

She got in and he closed the door behind her. When she looked up at him, his fingers touching the window, for the very first time she saw fear in his eyes.

Tuesday, July 16

ISAAC DROVE ACROSS TOWN, A little smile dancing across his face. He was listening to the boys jabbering away brightly about anything and everything—baseball, someone's birthday, a party that's coming up—just normal stuff that teenagers could talk about in front of a parent. Isaac's son Lucas rode in the front seat, his friends John Harris and Eric Hashimoto in the back, heading home from baseball practice at Wilson Park. The boys were teammates, first in high school and now on the American Legion team. But more than that, they were friends. Isaac marveled at how easy they made it look. It was way beyond his experience: growing up in the segregated South, serving in a segregated army unit during the war, living now in a de facto segregated neighborhood. Times were changing and these kids were going to lead the way, making their own decisions, choosing their friends, their associates—even their neighbors—for reasons that didn't involve color. He wondered if he could ever catch up. He turned left onto Cedar Street, then a quick left again into the Hashimotos' driveway.

"Thanks for the ride, Mr. Washington." Eric said a quick goodbye to his buddies and headed for the front door.

Isaac backed out of the driveway onto Cedar, made a right at the corner and pulled up in front of the Harris's home. There was another "Thanks for the ride, Mr. Washington," and John Harris was waving goodbye.

Mr. Washington. Mr. Isaac Washington, R.N. He was having a hard time getting used to it. He had aced the exam, and even found a job at Vallejo General Hospital. Things were definitely looking up. He pulled away from the curb and started down the street, wondering what Millie had on the stove for dinner. Then he looked up at the rearview mirror and saw the flashing lights of the police cruiser behind him. He pulled over to the curb and stopped.

"Dad? Did you do something wrong?" Lucas looked back at the police car, then at his father.

"No . . . I'm sure it's nothing. I'll handle it." Isaac tried to sound confident. In his rearview mirror, he could see the officers sitting in the patrol car, one of them talking into a radio handset. After several minutes, the driver opened the door and Isaac saw him walking toward his vehicle, his image growing larger in the mirror. He rolled down the window and waited.

"License and registration, please." The officer stooped slightly, his eyes scanning the inside of the car.

Isaac reached for his wallet in his back pocket. As he did this, he saw the officer place his right hand on the gun in its holster. He took the license out of his wallet, removed the registration holder clipped to the sun visor, and handed them to the officer.

"Mr. Washington?"

"Yes."

"Is this your vehicle?"

"Yes."

"Remain in the vehicle. And keep your hands on the wheel where we can see them." The officer turned and walked back toward the cruiser.

"Dad, what's going on? Why are they doing this?"

"Just be cool, son. Be cool." He said it, but with very little conviction. Isaac Washington could feel his blood beginning to boil.

John Harris stepped off the bus, turned and stood at the curb until it pulled away, then started across the street toward his house, the second from the corner. He looked up to see the police cruiser, lights flashing, one officer standing a few feet away from the vehicle, covering the second officer who was in the process of patting down a tall, slender black man. The suspect's legs were spread apart, pulled back, hands out against the vehicle. A second black man, younger, possibly late teens, also stood with his hands on the vehicle, waiting his turn to be frisked. John recognized the young man: it was Lucas Washington. And the older man was his father, Isaac. John also recognized the police officer covering his partner: it was Tom Wolf, the son of a man John worked with on the shipyard. All of this was happening a few yards down the block from the Harris' home. John reached the walk leading to his front door and called to the young officer.

"Tommy . . . hey, Tommy." The officer looked around and nodded in recognition. "What's goin' on?"

"Hey, Mr. Harris. Not much. Just a routine stop."

"A routine stop for what?"

"Well, we've had some break-ins in the neighborhood and this guy fits the description."

"Break-ins? I haven't heard of any break-ins."

"Well, let's just say they're a little out of place here." He turned and winked at John.

"Goddamn, Tommy, I know this man. That's Ike Washington. Our kids play ball together."

John Jr. came out of the house and stood next to his father. "Dad, why are they stopping Mr. Washington? He just dropped me off from practice."

"Hear that, Tommy? Ike just gave my kid a ride home from ball practice."

The officer named Tom looked annoyed, but called out to his partner who was finished patting down Isaac Washington. The second officer approached his partner and they had a quick, animated conversation.

"Okay, Mr. Harris, we're going to let 'em go, based on you vouched for 'em." Tom addressed Big John while his partner returned Isaac's license and registration. "You know, we would've turned 'em loose earlier, but he copped an attitude with us."

A few seconds later, the police cruiser swung around Isaac's car and hurried away, as if another urgent call had come in. John walked toward Isaac who was leaning back against his car, fighting to control his rage.

"Geez, Ike, sorry about that. You'd think they'd have something better to do."

"Oh . . . not a damn problem, Big John. Matter of fact, I'm getting used to it, starting to enjoy the damn pat-downs. Know what I mean? What the hell did you say to 'em?"

"Just that I know you, that you were dropping off my kid, that I could vouch for you."

"Vouch for me? Vouch for me, so that I can drive down the goddamn street? I did not know that I needed to be vouched for to drive in this neighborhood. Well . . . thank you Mr. John Harris." Isaac could feel the blood pulsing at his temples, feel his fists clenched tightly against the side of the car.

John felt awful. He knew there was nothing he could do to salvage the situation. Still, he had to try. "Ike, why don't you come on in and have a cold beer with me, let yourself calm down a little?"

Isaac looked at John Harris for a moment, and then burst into laughter. It was just too damn funny! *A beer? Come on in and have a beer? I'll bet that would be a first: the first nigger to set foot in that household—except for a maid.* And then he saw that John was dead serious. He stifled a new burst of laughter, and he felt his anger begin to subside.

"Well, I'll be . . . thanks, John . . . but Millie's got dinner on the stove. I think Lucas and I better head for home."

He called to his son who had wandered off to talk to John Jr. A minute later, they were on their way home, back to their neighborhood, safe among their own kind.

Wednesday, August 28

T HE SMALL CROWD AT THE bar sat mesmerized as they gazed
  at the images on the television screen, alternating between
shots of the activities inside the convention hall and rioting in the
streets of Chicago. In front of the Hilton Hotel, the police in their
light blue shirts and helmets were charging into the demonstrators,
nightsticks flying, while the demonstrators heaved rocks and
bottles and bags of urine in the direction of the police.

Inside the convention center, Senator Abraham Ribicoff was
at the podium, nominating George McGovern for president, using
the national stage to denounce ". . . Gestapo tactics in the streets
of Chicago." The Illinois delegation, seated right down front and
led by Mayor Richard Daley, shouted back at Ribicoff, inviting
him to go home—or go something.

Back in front of the Hilton, the demonstrators were chanting,
"The whole world is watching." They were right. And to the
world—including the regulars at Skip's Place—it seemed that
America had gone crazy.

"Can you believe that shit? I say 'go police,' bust some heads.
Who the hell are these people?"

"Did you see Daley? Did he just say 'fuck you' to Ribicoff?"

"Damn, I think you're right."

"Well, the Democrats just gave the damn election to the GOP.
Humphrey hasn't got a chance now."

"Hey, you never know. A lot can happen between now and
November."

"Are you kidding me? Nixon will eat this up. He'll beat 'em over the head with 'law and order' and they'll run these film clips over and over again."

"I feel for old Hubert. He's not such a bad guy."

"Oh, gimme a break. He's a dinosaur from the New Deal days. A bleeding heart liberal. All he wants to do is take your money and give it out to a bunch of welfare queens."

"He's not that bad. He had some good ideas—like the Peace Corps. Wasn't that his brainchild?"

"Big deal. Anyway, Nixon is gonna kick his ass, you wait and see."

"Shoot, I thought Nixon was dead back in '62. Remember his speech? 'You won't have Dick Nixon to kick around anymore.'"

"You can't keep a good man down. Besides, nobody understands politics in this country better than Dick Nixon."

"Ah . . . I don't trust a guy that wants it that bad."

"I think he'll be a good president. And I like this guy Agnew, too."

"That sonofabitch? I think he bites the heads off of puppies." (laughter)

Back in the streets, the whole world continued to watch as the police cracked heads with wild enthusiasm. For every demonstrator who dared to stand his ground, there seemed to be two cops ready to whack him—or her. And somewhere out there, Richard Milhous Nixon was watching and waiting.

Saturday, September 7

J OHN HARRIS RINSED HIS COFFEE mug and left it in the kitchen sink. He went looking for Martha to tell her he was leaving, heading down the street and around the corner for a haircut. He found his wife folding clothes in the bedroom.

"Okay, hon, I'm gonna go get a haircut. Should be back in an hour or so." He gave Martha a quick kiss on the cheek and headed for the front door.

John knew there would be a wait on a Saturday morning, but that was okay. He enjoyed the chance to sit and shoot the bull in the neighborhood barbershop. It was a beautiful September morning, clear and sunny, a real Indian summer day. He took his time strolling down the block, checking his neighbors' houses and yards as he went, looking for changes in landscaping or paint, perhaps a new car parked in a driveway. He was pleased with what he saw: the neighborhood was holding up pretty well. He rounded the corner on Georgia Street and headed for Barney's Barber Shop, situated in the collection of small storefronts anchored by a mom-and-pop market.

As John approached the shop, he saw the door swing open and a short compact figure burst out onto the walkway, closing the door with a bang. He recognized Kenji Hashimoto and started to call out to him. Kenji turned sharply and marched away, head down, eyes fixed on the pavement, clearly upset about something.

John opened the door and stepped into the shop. The two chairs were occupied and three customers were waiting. The lively conversation slowed just a bit as John came in.

"Hey, Big John! Time to get your ears lowered?" It was Barney with his usual greeting.

"Yeah, sure . . ." John was still puzzled by Kenji's rapid exit.

"Well, you missed all the excitement. We just had a Jap in here, looking for a haircut. I told him we don't serve Japs, that we remember Pearl Harbor. Right, guys?" This drew a murmur of approval from the other men.

"You mean Ken . . . I mean Kenji Hashimoto? Hell, he's my neighbor."

"The hell you say? Your neighbor? Since when do we have Japs in this neighborhood?"

John ignored the question. He exchanged hellos with the waiting customers, picked up a magazine and took a seat. The conversation moved to other topics—sports, politics, pretty women—and Kenji Hashimoto was forgotten for the time being, by all except John. He felt a sense of unease that he couldn't explain. Time passed, the chairs turned over, customers paid and left, calling their goodbyes on the way out the door.

Suddenly the door swung open, the bell attached to the door jam ringing brightly. Kenji stepped into the shop and approached Barney's chair, glaring up at the slightly taller man. John could see that he was wearing an Army uniform jacket, and he could see a military medal pinned to the breast. He recognized it as a Purple Heart.

"See this?" Kenji pointed to the medal. "Ever see one of these? I got mine in Italy, 1945, fighting for Uncle Sam. Where were you during the war, asshole? So you remember Pearl Harbor? I'll tell you what I remember: Monte Cassino in Italy, Biffontaine in France. That's what I remember."

The shop went dead silent. Barney stared at the medal, then looked at Kenji. The silence continued for several seconds. Finally, Barney spoke up. "Look, friend, I made a mistake. I didn't know. If you want to take a seat, I'll be glad to cut your hair."

Kenji moved closer, inches from Barney's face, as though he were ready to take a bite out of the man. "I wouldn't let you cut my hair if it was free—for life." He turned and walked out of the shop, closing the door hard as he went.

"Well, I'll be . . ." Barney could think of nothing more to say. John dropped the magazine on the table and headed toward the door. "Hey, John, you're not staying? You'll be up soon."

"Nah, Barney. Not today. Maybe later." He left the shop and headed for home.

John opened the front door and went straight to the kitchen. He had a pretty good idea where he'd find Kenji Hashimoto. He looked out the kitchen window, across the low picket fence at the back of the property, and sure enough, there was Kenji sitting on the stone bench by his rock garden. John opened the refrigerator, took out a couple of bottles of Falstaff and headed for the backyard.

"Hey, Kenji, mind if I join you?" Kenji looked up and thought seriously about building a taller fence. He motioned for John to come over. John approached the bench and held out one of the bottles. "I don't have any of that good Jap beer, but at least it's cold."

Kenji looked up, saw the half-smile on John's face and knew he was being messed with. He accepted the beer. He moved over and patted the bench for John to sit down.

"So, you served in Italy and France? How did that happen?"

"I was with the 442nd Regimental Combat Team. All Japanese, mostly from Hawaii, but about 800 of us from the U.S. internment camps. They came around at Rohwer and asked for volunteers."

John had heard of the 442nd RCT, the "Go For Broke" regiment, *the* most decorated unit in the Army. "And you signed up? I heard of lot of guys refused, even renounced their citizenship."

"There was a lot of anger, John. Some guys renounced. Others said they'd volunteer if their families were released and their full rights were restored."

"But you volunteered. Why? Your family was locked up. You were moved across the country. Why volunteer, for God's sake?"

Kenji glared at John, a look of pure defiance and pride. "Because this is my country too. My parents are Nisei; they were born here. I was born here. I'm every bit as American as Franklin Delano Roosevelt, or Earl Warren, or General John Fucking DeWitt!" He looked away, fighting for composure. More than twenty years and it was still an open wound.

"I saw the Purple Heart. Where did you get hit?"

Kenji rubbed his right leg. Thinking about it always seemed to make it hurt. "I took some shrapnel in my right leg. Nothing too serious. Just bad enough to get me shipped home. The 442nd was back in Italy, 1945. The fighting was almost over anyway."

John looked at Kenji and pondered everything he'd learned about the Hashimoto family and what the war had done to them. "Damn," he said, "and now my friend Barney doesn't want to cut your hair. Well, Mr. Hashimoto, you and I are going to have to find a new barbershop."

Kenji laughed in spite of himself. He and Big John clinked bottles and drank deeply of the fine American beer.

Wednesday, September 11

B OBBIE PULLED HER CAR INTO the space next to John's, killed the engine and turned out the lights. John was standing next to the railing that ran along the walkway overlooking the Mare Island Strait, the lights of the shipyard burning brightly across the water, the balmy fall air filled with the clank and bang of steel being transformed into warships. Bobbie joined him at the railing where they exchanged a quick hug and a kiss.

"Thanks for coming, Johnny. I wanted to talk to you in person."

"You look great, Bobbie. Is that a new shirt?" She always looked great to John, but especially tonight, wearing a new dashiki, tight fitting jeans and tall leather boots. The clothes, the jewelry, the regal bearing—it all came together to stir John's feelings for her.

"I want to tell you right away, Johnny, I'm not pregnant. I got my period this morning, just out of the blue. I would have told you earlier but I didn't want to do it on the phone."

"Geez, Bobbie, I don't know what to say. I mean, that's good, right? You're okay? Heck, *we're* okay!"

He put his arms around her and held her close for a minute or so. A great feeling of relief washed over him. They stepped away from the rail, holding hands, and began to walk south along the waterfront.

Just then, a police cruiser pulled into the parking lot and drove toward them, the headlights glaring in their eyes. The vehicle came to a stop and they could hear the crackle of the two-way radio inside the car. The doors opened and the officers stepped out of the car; the driver approached, giving them a quick nod of his head.

"What's your business here, folks?"

"We're just talking, officer . . ." John wasn't sure what more to say.

"Are these your vehicles?"

"Yes, sir."

"Okay, I want the two of you to return to your vehicles. I'll need to see license and registration." The first officer, the one who had been driving, went with Bobbie while the second officer approached John. Two very different conversations ensued. While John produced his license and registration, Bobbie was having a different experience.

"Where is your license, miss?"

"In the car . . . in my purse."

"Bring the purse out here where I can see it. Do you have any weapons, anything sharp in there?"

"No—"

"Okay, open it so I can see inside." He pointed a long flashlight into the large, floppy handbag and scanned the contents. "Whoa, what is that?"

"What? Oh, that's a comb . . . a hair pick . . . for my hair."

"Nothing sharp, eh? Okay, take it out and set it on the hood." She did as he asked. "Now your drivers license." She opened her wallet and retrieved the license. "And registration." She pulled the small holder containing the document from the sun visor and handed it to him. "Is this your vehicle?"

"It's my father's."

"Name and address?" She provided the information and the officer seemed satisfied. "Again, what's your business here? Is this your regular stroll?"

It dawned on Bobbie that she'd been pegged as a prostitute. Of course! A black girl walking the waterfront with a white boy: a new generation of the world's oldest profession.

"There's no business . . . we were just talking . . . he's my boyfriend."

"I'll bet he is."

"Look, I'm not a hooker—" She was beginning to see red now.

"Don't give me attitude, miss. This is a high crime area. More prostitutes than we can count. So no attitude, got it! Stay here while we check you out." With that he walked back to the patrol car to confer with his partner.

"What do you think?"

"Hell, I think they're just lovebirds. Salt 'n pepper style. Let's turn 'em loose and move on."

"What's a nice white boy want with a soul sister, anyway?"

"Hey, did you get a look at her? She's a fox. Hell, I'd do her."

"Hell, you'd do anything female. That's why your daddy won't let you around the sheep anymore."

"Screw you, too. I'm just saying, I'd like to pat her down. She's got a nice lookin' ass."

"Shit, just give 'em back their IDs and let's get out of here."

The patrol car pulled away, leaving them in a state of shock, and in Bobbie's case, rage.

"So that's it, Johnny. If you're a black girl in this part of town with a white boy, you must be a whore. Right?"

"Bobbie, calm down . . . they're gone now . . . it's okay."

"Sure it's okay. This is where we live, Johnny. The land of the free and the home of the brave. Where all men are created equal. America the beautiful."

"Okay . . . okay . . . I know you're upset."

"Go home, Johnny." She opened her car door and got in. "Go on home to your neighborhood and I'll go home to mine." She was choking back tears now. "And just be damn happy that you're not going to be the father of a little brown baby."

The tires screeched as she backed away from the curb, then again as she sped away, leaving John to feel like a hapless piece of shit.

Sunday, October 6

E LLAMAE HURRIED INTO THE LITTLE church, pausing to say hello to friends as she passed, heading toward her customary seat near the front of the sanctuary. She loved sitting up front where she could enjoy the choir and see their expressions change as the music moved them. And she didn't want to miss a word of the sermon delivered by Rev. Booker T. Redman, affectionately known as "Boomer" among his congregants. Boomer Redman was blessed with a magnificent voice, a rolling *basso profundo* that could rattle the stained glass windows and carry out into the parking lot. When he spoke the word of God, no one dozed off.

Isaac Washington and his family—Millie, Bobbie and Lucas—greeted Ellamae warmly, making room for her in the well-worn oak pew. She looked around for her son Julian and his wife Angie and saw them approaching from the center aisle to envelop her with hugs. They chatted for a few minutes, waiting for the service to begin. The sanctuary was packed as usual, the ushers moving about, encouraging people to squeeze closer together, making room for new arrivals.

And then a hush fell over the congregation as Rev. Redman appeared at the back of the room, his simple black robe like a tent around his ample body, his Bible tucked firmly under his right arm, the choir in their bright gold robes queued up behind him. He sounded the call to worship in that wonderful voice and led the procession down the center isle as the choir began the hymn "Shall We Gather At The River." Ellamae felt a little chill go up her spine. This scene, witnessed so many times, never failed to move her. *God, bless this house and all within.*

The service proceeded as usual: several hymns, a scripture lesson, a rousing performance by the choir, announcements from the current president of the congregation, and finally, it was time for the sermon.

Rev. Redman stepped to the pulpit and it was clear that he was a troubled man this day. His brow was furrowed, his lips pinched together tightly, as though someone or some thing had hit him in the gut. He adjusted the microphone, though he probably didn't need it, raised his eyes to look out upon his flock, and began:

> "Where have all the flowers gone?/Long time passing..."
>
> So goes the folk song popular a few years ago. The song teaches us the answer: Young girls pick the flowers. The young girls go to young men. The young men go for soldiers. Soldiers go to graveyards. Graveyards go to flowers. And so, the cycle is completed, only to begin again ... and again. We are left with the haunting question: "When will we ever learn?"
>
> Just a simple little song. Or is it? We look around our community today and we see the story set in motion: Young men taken from among us, caught in the draft, or enlisting to avoid it, and then—gone for soldiers, every one.
>
> Are these young men the children of the Upper Class? Are they the children of the prosperous Middle Class? Or, my brothers and sisters, are they primarily the children of the working poor? In other words, *our children!*
>
> Young men from the barrios and ghettos of our cities, sons of coal miners in rural Appalachia and sharecroppers in the Deep South, black and brown—and yes—white. *Our* young men, *our children.* Gone for soldiers, every one.
>
> With money and influence, there are options to consider: college deferment; conscientious objector

status; a rare spot in the Reserve or National Guard. And if all else fails, leave the country. Head north to the bosom of our friends in Canada.

The recruiters flock to our neighborhoods. Enlist, they say, and you can learn a useful skill. Enlist and there will be money for college when you get out. Never mind that your school system left you reading at a fourth grade level. Enlist for the promise of a brighter future.

When you come home, we'll take care of you. The VA will see to your needs. We won't leave you to the streets, with alcohol on your breath and needle tracks on your arms. We won't leave you to be spat upon and called *baby killer*. Trust us. Sign here.

Brothers and sisters, look around you. Look at the young men sent home with broken minds and bodies, fending for themselves out on the streets, the only useful skill they've been taught: to kill or be killed.

I say to you it is time for the cycle to end, time for our young men to soldier no more, time to end the perpetuation of the Warrior Class culled from the families of the working poor, cannon fodder for the war machine.

It is time to say, *Hell no, we won't go.* Time to answer the age-old question: "When will we ever learn?" Amen.

This was not a typical sermon for Rev. Redman. He generally stayed close to home, basing his message on the day's scripture lesson as it applied to life in the 20th century. His preference was to leave politics to the politicians. His message this day caught the congregation off guard. Of course, there had been the customary cries of "Amen" during the sermon, offered up to punctuate the traditional call-and-response style. But Boomer Redman had been oddly subdued in his delivery, raising his voice only to punctuate *our children* and *Hell no, we won't go.* His final line—*When will we ever learn?*—was delivered just above a whisper. The overall impact was stunning: his message had been driven home with the intensity of a sledgehammer.

Outside the church, the people lingered on the lawn and in the parking lot, visiting and laughing, making plans for the coming week, sharing thoughts and opinions. Not everyone agreed with the Reverend's message. After all, this was a town that depended on the military, and several men in the congregation had served proudly in World War II and in Korea. They tended to see Vietnam as the responsibility of the current generation. It was time for the young folks to step up and do their part. And yet, Rev. Redman had given them something to think about.

Isaac Washington stood quietly with his family, mulling over several phrases that stuck in his mind. *Warrior Class . . . cannon fodder . . . war machine.* Is that what the old, gray men who made decisions about war and peace were doing? Creating a self-perpetuating Warrior Class? Isaac shuddered involuntarily. He looked at his son Lucas, standing just a few feet away. *One year . . . just one year from now he'll have to register for the draft.*

Bobbie was thinking about John Harris, Jr. He was likely to receive an athletic scholarship, and with it, the coveted student deferment. That was good. But what about Lucas? And what about Thaddeus Brown? She knew Thad had finished basic training, and then combat training, but she wasn't sure about his next posting. She looked for Thad's father Julian and saw him standing across the lawn with his mother. She saw that Ellamae was dabbing her eyes, clinging tightly to her son, and she could sense it was not the right time to ask about Thad.

Ellamae stood with her right arm wrapped around Julian's waist. His left arm was around her shoulders, holding her close. There was nothing much to say, and Ellamae could not stop the tears from falling. They stood there in the bright sunshine, dealing quietly with the latest news: Thaddeus was on his way to Vietnam, to a place called Da Nang. *Dear Lord, watch over that child and keep him from harm.*

Wednesday, October 16

T HEY STOOD ON THE PODIUM at the Olympic Stadium in Mexico City, the three medal winners in the 200-meter dash: Tommy Smith and John Carlos of the United States with the gold and bronze medals respectively, Peter Norman of Australia with the silver. As the Star Spangled Banner began to play and the flags rose slowly over the stadium, Smith and Carlos each raised a black-gloved fist high in the air—Smith his right, Carlos his left—and they closed their eyes and bowed their heads.

To the north, in cities all across America, cries of shock and outrage were directed at television screens as the message hit home. These two young black men were making a statement, and using the biggest stage in the world to deliver it.

The regulars down at Skip's Place reacted in typical fashion, which is to say with a mixed bag of anger and—perhaps surprisingly—grudging support.

"Did you see that? What the hell was that?"

"Some sort of black power salute, or something."

"Well, I'll be goddamned! We send these kids down there, pay their way, feed 'em, house 'em, provide the best coaches in the world, and what do they do? They spit in our faces!"

"They ought to kick their asses off the team, and make 'em pay their own way home, the sonsabitches. What gives them the right?"

"What gives them the right? They're American citizens, for God's sake. It's called free speech."

"Oh, don't give me that. It's the wrong place and the wrong time. This is crap. And what do these guys have to protest anyway?"

"Hey, we still got a long way to go, man. In jobs and housing especially. Tell me this: could a black man buy a house in your neighborhood? Could he belong to your union?"

"Ah, you friggin' liberals give me a pain. They've got every opportunity in this country. Let them do just like the Irish and the Italians and the Jews did: get out there and work for it."

"It's that damn Harry Edwards down there at Cal that got 'em all worked up. You know he wanted all black athletes to boycott the games?"

"Let's face it: we wouldn't have much of a team without them. Hell, Smith set a new world record."

"Did you hear that? They just said Avery Brundage suspended them from the team and he wants them out of the Olympic Village."

"Serves 'em right."

"Brundage says political statements have no place in the Olympics."

"Oh really? Where was he in 1936 in Berlin? No political statements, my ass! If it isn't political, then why do they play national anthems?"

The reporters covering the Olympic Games were digging hard now, trying to get out in front of the story. Before long, the details came pouring out, fueling the controversy. Tommy Smith said his black-gloved fist represented black power, while John Carlos's represented black unity. Both men stood on the podium in black sox—and no shoes—to represent black poverty in racist America. All three athletes, including Peter Norman, wore badges representing Harry Edwards's Olympic Project for Civil Rights.

No one—neither reporters nor athletes nor fans—could anticipate the shit storm that would rain down on these three young men, or the impact that it would have on the rest of their lives.

Friday, October 25

T HE CROWD MILLED AROUND OUTSIDE the stadium, gathered in groups, talking and laughing, beginning to line up and file past the ticket booths. Corbus Field would be packed tonight for the game against Sir Francis Drake High, one of those upscale Marin schools. Friday night football always drew a great crowd—parents, faculty and students—to see the Vallejo High Apaches play. Inside the stadium, the band was warming up with a rousing rendition of the theme from "Peter Gunn."

John Harris loved the Friday night football scene. It was a great way to end the week and the glow of a victory always carried through the weekend. His wife Martha and daughter Jenny were with him, bundled up in several layers of clothing against the cool October night, carrying blankets to spread on the hard wooden bench seats. John and Martha would sit with the other team parents, in a section right below the press box. Jenny would be off with her friends, here there and everywhere around the massive concrete grandstand.

They made their way up the steep steps toward the press box, pausing to chat with friends along the way. Near the top, John saw Kenji and Tami Hashimoto seated next to Isaac and Millie Washington and he gave them a wave. Lucas Washington was the starting tailback and a fine runner, Eric Hashimoto the starting center. John Harris, Jr. was a linebacker, anchoring a solid defensive unit. They found an open space next to the Hashimotos and spread their blankets.

The Drake squad was already on the field going through its warm-up routine. Out across the field, where the buildings of the campus were clustered on a rise behind the stadium, they saw the Vallejo team file out of Bottari Gym, heading in a long line toward the gate on the east side of the stadium. At a signal from across the field, the bass drummer in the band took up the tom-tom beat—BOOM boom boom boom/BOOM boom boom boom—and the Apaches ran onto the field in single file, led by their captains. The team arrayed into a grid at the north end of the field to begin their warm-ups as the band went into the "Indian War Chant." Finally, with the warm-up drills well underway, the band segued into a spirited version of "Cherokee." This little ritual always sent chills up John Harris's spine, and he was sure he wasn't the only one.

Now as it neared time for the kick-off, the Vallejo cheerleaders mounted the platform in front of the student section to lead the "Hello" yell:

> *Oh, Drake has got a battleship*
> *They've also got a bell*
> *But Vallejo's got a submarine*
> *To blow 'em all to*
> *Hell-O, Dra-ake.*

Vallejo kicked off to Drake and the game was underway, the rolling baritone voice of Lou Sanders on the PA system, calling the plays: "Smith the ball carrier, brought down by Harris. Gain of three yards. Second down." The crowd settled in for the long battle, joining the cheerleaders in all the familiar yells: "We've got a T-E-A-M/It's on the B-E-A-M." Or, "Victory, victory, that's our cry. V-I-C-T-O-R-Y . . ."

Drake marched down the field, scored a touchdown, but missed the extra point. Vallejo answered with a drive of its own, Lucas Washington breaking off a nineteen yard run for the touchdown. The extra point was good and the band went into the Vallejo fight song:

Onward Apaches, fight fight fight
Lead us to victory, men
We're on the warpath
Scalping to win
Ring up the score again
Vallejo . . .

After that, the game settled into a defensive struggle, and when the gun sounded for the end of the first half, Vallejo led seven to six. John Harris headed for the snack bar located under the grandstand, daughter Jenny pulling him along, insisting that a hot dog and a Coke were all that stood between her and starvation. Holding the cups of coffee he'd purchased for himself and Martha, he stopped to visit with friends while Jenny bounded up the steps to enjoy her hotdog and watch the cheerleaders perform their half time routines.

Suddenly, John felt someone tugging at his sleeve. "Mr. Harris, you'd better come quick. Something's wrong with Jenny."

Without stopping to think, John tossed the cups of coffee into a nearby trashcan and hurried up the steps to the grandstand. He glanced up to the section below the press box and saw a small crowd gathered there. He ran up the aisle, taking the steps two at a time, gasping for breath. He burst into the group surrounding Martha and Jenny, and what he saw terrified him. His daughter's face was turning purple, her hands clutching her throat, her eyes wide with terror as she struggled to breathe. Behind her, Isaac Washington held her with one arm and slapped her back hard with the flat of his hand.

"Ike, what are you doing?" John could barely get the words out.

"Wait, let me try this."

Isaac wrapped both arms around Jenny from behind, made a fist just below her rib cage, and pulled in hard. Nothing happened. He pulled hard again, and this time a small, round projectile shot from Jenny's mouth, landing on the bench three feet away. Jenny gasped as her lungs began to function again, air rushing in and out. Isaac let her go and she fell into her mother's arms, sobbing, her head buried against Martha's shoulder, her normal color coming back swiftly.

Isaac picked up the projectile that Jenny had spit out, an inch long section of hot dog. "See here? The perfect plug. The abdominal compressions did the trick, thank God."

A doctor who'd been sitting nearby came into their circle and spent a few minutes examining Jenny. He said she seemed fine, but he suggested that they take her home and keep an eye on her, perhaps call their family doctor and hear his advice. The Hashimotos offered to give John Jr. a ride home after the game, and with that, the Harrises headed for the exit. The second half was just underway as they reached the parking lot.

John opened the kitchen cupboard and reached for the bottle of Jack Daniel's on the upper shelf. He took down two water glasses and poured a couple of fingers of the amber liquid into each of them. Martha entered the kitchen and John offered her a drink, which she promptly accepted.

"She's sound asleep, like nothing ever happened." Martha took the glass from John and swirled the whiskey around the bottom of the glass. She looked at John, standing a few feet away, leaning against the countertop, and then her composure crumbled, the tears streaming down her face. John took her in his arms and held her close, her body racked with sobs. "We almost lost her, John. We almost lost her."

"Yeah, I know," he said quietly, rocking her gently in his arms. "Thank God Ike Washington was there."

Sunday, November 3

"S O, HOW WAS THE TRIP? Did you like the campus?"

"Yeah, it was nice . . . beautiful, actually. And the training facilities are amazing . . ." John's voice on the phone was flat, hesitant, not at all what Bobbie expected.

"Uh huh . . . what else, Johnny? Did you meet some of the guys on the team?"

"Yeah, I met a bunch of the guys . . . they seem real nice."

"Come on, Johnny, you don't sound very excited. What's wrong?"

"Nothing, Bobbie . . . I mean it's a great offer—basically a full ride scholarship for football. And I can walk on to tryout for the baseball team if I want."

"It sounds perfect, Johnny! Why aren't you happy about this?"

John had just returned from an official recruiting visit to UCLA. He and his father had spent the weekend touring the campus, meeting prospective teammates, and talking to the coaching staff. The scholarship offer was on the table now. All he had to do was sign the Letter of Intent and he would be on his way to a future that had no limits.

"I don't know, Bobbie . . . I'm not sure I want to be in L.A., four hundred miles away, and you back here in Vallejo. I mean, I could go to the JC and play football there, and baseball too. At least we could see each other, be together. Ya know?"

A sudden hollow feeling gripped Bobbie's stomach. This was not good. She had to do something, and do it fast.

"Okay, look Johnny, we need to talk face-to-face. Can you meet me somewhere? How about Scotty's? We really need to talk."

Bobbie drove across town, heading for the corner of Tennessee and Tuolumne, the site of Scotty's Doughnuts, a Vallejo institution. She was thinking hard and fast, trying to sort out her feelings. She and John had fallen back into their relationship following the pregnancy scare, taking pains to be more careful than ever before. Bobbie saw a physician and obtained a prescription for the pill. There was no question that they were in love, and yet she knew she was holding something back, never quite letting go. She'd known all along that this day was coming. Now she would have to find a way to convince him, even if she had to hurt him in the process. She could not let him walk away from his future.

Bobbie thought about the letter she had received from her cousin Thad, serving in Vietnam. What was the acronym he had used to describe the situation there? FUBAR—Fucked Up Beyond All Recognition. She knew she had to prevent their situation from going FUBAR.

They met at Scotty's, but wound up sitting in John's car in the parking lot rather than going into the shop. Bobbie wasted no time getting directly to the issue.

"Listen to me, Johnny. You've got to sign that Letter of Intent, you've got to accept the scholarship."

"I don't know, Bobbie. What I really want is to be here with you."

"I know, baby, I know . . . but listen to me. We both have to move on with our lives. Remember I told you I wanted to go back to school when I saved some money? Well, I've decided to go back to Sacramento. I can live with my old roommate, and there's a nursing program I can get into up there. I want to be a nurse and do what my daddy's doing."

She was lying through her teeth now. Not that nursing was a bad idea. In fact, it was a move she'd been thinking about for some time, though the plan was not nearly as well formed as she was presenting it.

She went on: "I can start the program in January, Johnny. I'm going to give notice at my job soon. So you see, baby, I won't be here. There's no point in you staying in Vallejo, 'cause I'll be gone."

"Geez, Bobbie, I didn't know you were thinking about going back—"

"Look, Johnny . . ." Her voice caught in her throat now. She was going to be brutally honest with him. "You've just started your senior year in high school. You've got the best year of your life ahead of you: all the big dances, the Prom, the senior picnic, graduation, the all-night party, all of those once-in-a-lifetime experiences. And I can't share any of that with you. We need to move on with our lives. You need to go to UCLA. UCLA, Johnny! Do you know what it means to get a degree from the University of California? And I need to get on with my life. I have dreams, too, baby."

She went on, making her case, knowing that her argument was bulletproof. Before long they were both in tears. Plain and simple, she was breaking up with him, urging him to embrace the life of a normal high school senior, and to commit for next fall to a university located four hundred miles away. Bobbie knew she was winning this debate; at the same time, she was losing the boy she loved. Then again, she'd known from the very beginning that it would end this way.

Finally, she left his car and headed for her own, tears clouding her vision. She knew without question that she'd done the right thing. Why then did it feel so FUBAR?

Tuesday, November 5

A small Tuesday night crowd gathered at Skip's, watching the election returns trickle in, waiting for one of the three major networks to declare a winner. After a while, they grew bored with the coverage and Skip switched to a channel showing *I Love Lucy* reruns; that is, until the polls closed in California. Then it was back to Skip's favorite network, CBS, where he expected to hear the straight scoop from the veteran team anchored by Walter Cronkite. Little did Skip and his customers know that they'd have to wait until Wednesday morning for a winner to be declared.

"I can't believe it's this close. Humphrey was so far behind coming out of Chicago in August, I didn't think it was possible for him to make up the ground."

"Yeah, but he waited too long to break with Johnson and come out for an end to the bombing. He should have done that right off the bat."

"And what about Nixon? Losing to Kennedy in '60. Losing for governor in '62. I thought he was dead. What a comeback!"

"You know, I think he'll be a pretty good president."

The lone woman sitting at the bar spoke up then, her voice heavy with emotion. "Ah, they're all a bunch of crooks . . . a bunch of lousy crooks, every damn one of 'em."

"Come on, Alice, why do you say that?"

"Because it's true. Look what they do: stage some phony Gulf of Tonkin incident so they can bomb North Vietnam. Send five hundred thousand of our kids to prop up those crooks in Saigon.

And then, at the last minute, a week before the election, Johnson declares a halt to the bombing and says a peace agreement is close, just to try to throw the election to Humphrey."

"Well, hell—"

"Do you think LBJ cares about the kids that are dying while he plays politics with their lives? He doesn't give a rat's ass! All they care about is power. They'll do anything to get it, and they'll do anything to keep it."

"Hey, calm down, Alice. Come on—"

She was crying openly now. "My best friend just lost her son. He's coming home in a box. And for what? Half the country is against the damn war. They're all a bunch of crooks."

"Well, Nixon says he's got a secret plan to end the war."

"And you believe that crap? If he's got a plan, why doesn't he tell us what it is? And what about Humphrey? He didn't come out for a bombing halt until he saw he was getting his ass kicked in the polls. They're a bunch of damn crooks."

"You know, Alice may be right. Remember that Orson Welles film, where his character Harry Lime is way up in a Ferris wheel or something, and he says to Joseph Cotton, 'See those people down there, all those little black dots? If one of those dots stopped moving forever, would you really care?' That's our politicians, up there in that Ferris wheel, looking down at all of us little black dots on the ground."

"Well, listen to you, Mr. Philosopher. Since when did you get so intellectual? Orson Welles, my ass—"

Their attention returned to the election results.

"Hey, how 'bout George Wallace? Looks like he is going to carry about five states: Georgia, Alabama, Louisiana, Mississippi and Arkansas."

"Geez, Humphrey could really use those electoral votes."

"Hell, those votes were never going to Humphrey. They would have gone to Nixon. The old 'solid South' hates the Democrats now, because of the civil rights laws."

"Wallace was never going to win the election. What was he trying to do?"

"He wanted to keep Humphrey and Nixon from getting two hundred and seventy electoral votes, throw the election into the House of Representatives."

"How the hell does that work anyway? Since they're mostly Democrats, wouldn't they just vote for Humphrey?"

"Damned if I know. I'm sure if it looks like it's going that way, Uncle Walter will explain it to us."

And so it went as the clock ticked closer to midnight. Alice's friends took her home. Skip resisted the temptation to switch channels in search of something to laugh about. And eventually, Walter Cronkite advised his viewers that it was all coming down to Ohio, Illinois, and California—all three states too close to call. Nixon would wind up carrying those three states and the country would wake up to the news that he, Richard M. Nixon, would become the thirty-seventh president of the United States, winning three hundred and one votes in the Electoral College. The true election wonks noticed right away that if Humphrey had carried California, George Wallace would have achieved his goal.

Nixon's secret plan took another seven years to bear fruit. In the meantime, many more sons and daughters came home in flag draped coffins, black dots on the ground that simply stopped moving forever.

Monday, November 11

C ITY PARK AND THE SURROUNDING streets were packed. Everyone who would participate in the Veteran's Day parade was gathered, milling around, waiting to be organized. The parade committee was busy, walking through the noisy throng, making check marks on their ubiquitous clipboards, making sure all the elements were present and accounted for.

John Harris scanned the crowd and ran his own mental checklist. There were two high school bands, one from Vallejo and one from Armijo High in Fairfield. There was a mounted patrol on beautiful golden palominos. A dozen Shriners were present, each wearing a fez and driving one of those tiny cars. John saw the Navy color guard from Mare Island, carrying the Stars and Stripes, the Navy ensign, and the California Bear Flag. On the street, several convertibles were lined up, ready to transport the Grand Marshall, the mayor, and several pretty girls wearing sashes to proclaim their titles. And finally, there were the veterans who would march in loose formation behind the band from Vallejo High, some wearing their faded service uniforms and others, like John, in their VFW caps and jackets.

The parade route would take them south on Marin Street to Georgia, then west on Georgia Street through the main shopping district, and finally to Waterfront Park. There a platform had been erected and a sound system installed so that the mayor and other distinguished guests could say a few words. In between speakers, the two bands would trade numbers, each determined to outperform the other. It was a good plan and the committee was determined that it would be executed to perfection.

John saw a group of friends from the VFW post gathered in a circle, laughing and cutting up, and he wandered over to join them. One of the men was about to launch into a story and all eyes and ears were focused on the storyteller. As he started to speak, John saw Kenji Hashimoto and Isaac Washington standing together, just outside the circle, both of them wearing their old Army uniforms.

"So I have this buddy who runs a business," the storyteller began, "and he's got a couple of *schvartzes*—that's what he calls colored guys—working for him. So he sends the *schvartzes* out to make a delivery. It's about an hour there and an hour back and he figures they'll be gone two, maybe two and half hours. So they're gone a couple of hours and he gets a phone call. It's one of the *schvartzes*. He says, 'Mistuh Bernie, we went like you tol us, but we cain't find dat address. We dun drove up 'n down 'n round, and we is lost, Mistuh Bernie, we is jes flat lost.' And Bernie says, 'Hold the phone, Willie, hold the phone. Where are you?' Willie says, 'I's in a phone booth at dis big inner-secshun. They's cars flying by ever which way.' Bernie says, 'Okay, Willie, I want you look outside for the street signs. Tell me what the street signs say.' So the line goes quiet for a minute, then Willie comes back on. 'You's right, Mistuh Bernie, I dun seen the street signs.' Bernie says, 'Okay, Willie, that's great. What do the street signs say?' Willie says, 'They say *Walk* and *Don't Walk*. We is at the corner of *Walk* and *Don't Walk!*'"

The men gathered in the circle threw their heads back and howled with laughter; that is except for John Harris. John was looking at Isaac Washington's face, and now he felt a little sick to his stomach. He pushed through the group and made his way to where Isaac and Kenji were standing.

"What's the matter, Big John? You're not laughing. 'The corner of Walk and Don't Walk'? Now that's funny!" Isaac had a wry smile on his face.

Kenji picked up on the sarcasm. "Yeah, those darn *schvartzes!* Always good for a laugh."

"Ah, don't listen to that guy. He's a jerk. Say fellas, I have a proposition for you. I would be honored to march with you in the parade. And if you so honor me, I will buy you both a drink at Skip's Place when we get to the waterfront. Whataya say?"

Kenji and Isaac looked at each other and shrugged. "Hey, if Big John is opening his wallet, I'm not saying no." Isaac nodded in agreement.

"You think they'll serve a mixed trio like us, John? They might just throw us out on our cans." Isaac was into the spirit of it now.

"Who, Skip? Nah, Skip's a good guy. He takes all comers."

Just then, the head of the parade committee clicked on her bullhorn and began to bark directions. The lead elements of the parade fell into place out in the street—the banner carriers, the cars carrying the Grand Marshall and the local dignitaries, and the band from Armijo High. John saw a float roll past, a replica of the USS California, and he felt a large lump in his throat. There was nothing like the excitement that filled the air just before a parade stepped off. Then came a shrill blast from a whistle, a rousing drum roll, and the Armijo band broke into "Stars and Stripes Forever." The parade was underway, rolling up Marin Street.

As the sound of the band faded into the distance, the director clicked on her bullhorn again and ordered the veterans to queue up behind the Vallejo High band in their Apache red uniforms. The drum major split the air with a blast from his whistle, the corps of drummers went into a rousing eight bars that kicked off "Anchors Aweigh," and they began to march. John heard Navy veterans around him singing along with the band and he lent his booming voice to the chorus . . .

> Anchors aweigh, my boys
> Anchors aweigh . . .

The people who lined the street smiled and waved little flags as they marched past, and John could see that they were singing along as well; after all, this was a Navy town and damn proud of it. Then another whistle blast, another eight bars from the drummers, and now it was the Army's time to sing . . .

> *Over hill, over dale, we will hit the dusty trail*
> *As those caissons go rolling along . . .*

John looked at Isaac and Kenji, their heads held high, singing at the top of their lungs, calling out their numbers loud and strong. Along the street, they saw fathers with their children on their shoulders and mothers clutching their babies. Then another drum break and it was the flyboys turn . . .

> *Off we go, into the wild blue yonder*
> *Flying high, into the sun . . .*

They marched past old men in wheelchairs, wearing their VFW caps and saluting as they went by. The final break came and the Marines were more than ready, determined to be the boldest yet . . .

> *From the halls of Montezuma*
> *To the shores of Tripoli . . .*

John, Kenji, and Isaac looked at each other and grinned, their eyes wet with the pure emotion that filled the cool November air. Black, white, oriental—suddenly it didn't matter a whit. They were just three proud Americans, veterans and survivors of the bloodiest war in history, charter members of what would come to be known as The Greatest Generation.

Sunday, December 22

R UTH LEV SAT AT HER dining room table, preparing to light the candles on her *menorah*. This was the seventh night of *Chanukah*, and so she took eight of the small candles from the box—one for each day and one for the *shamas*—and placed them in their respective holders. She struck a match and lit the *shamas*, then used it to light the other candles in sequence. Finally, she replaced the *shamas* and began to recite the Hebrew blessings:

> "*Barukh attah Adonai*
> *Eloheinu melekh ha'olam*
> *Asher kidishanu b'mitz'votav*
> *V'tzivanu l'had'lik neir*
> *Shel Chanukah (Amein)*

> "*Barukh atah Adonai*
> *Eloheinu melekh ha'olam*
> *She'asah nisim la'avoteinu*
> *Bayamim haheim*
> *Baziman hazeh (Amein)*"

She watched quietly as the little candles burned, noting the colored wax that had dripped onto the *menorah*. Perhaps it was time to give it a good cleaning. And yet the thought of removing these remnants of *Chanukah* past repelled her. She just couldn't bring herself to do it.

Ruth had purchased this *menorah* at a Judaica shop in San Francisco shortly after arriving in the U.S. from Germany. She selected it because it was the closest she could find to the design of the one her parents had owned, the *menorah* she remembered from her childhood. It was nothing elaborate or expensive. It simply reminded her of home.

She watched the candles burn to the very end, the last piece of wick consuming the last bit of wax, a little puff of smoke rising from each candle to signal the end. Then Ruth did something unusual. She removed one more candle from the box, struck a match and lit it, and then placed in one of the holders. As she did this, she said a silent prayer for Milton Jacob Lev, her grandson. She tried her best to picture him somewhere up in the snowy plains north of Toronto. She prayed that he was warm and happy. She prayed that God would watch over him and keep him safe. She prayed that he would bring peace to Milton's troubled mind, and that one day soon he would come home safely. And again, she watched the candle burn until the tiny puff of smoke rose into the air.

Ruth wondered if this was kosher, if God would hear this prayer? She wasn't certain and there was no one to ask such a question. She believed one thing for sure: God owed her a few answers.

In North Korea, it was another day: December 23 to be exact. Captain Lloyd Bucher and the crew of the USS *Pueblo* were loaded onto buses and driven to the Demilitarized Zone that separates the two Koreas. There they were told to march south across the Bridge of No Return. Captain Bucher led the way, 82 men walking in single file, with Executive Officer Lieutenant Ed Murphy the last man to cross over to freedom.

This should have been the end of the ordeal for the men of the *Pueblo*, an ordeal marked by beatings, torture, mock firing squads, and public humiliation. It was also marked by defiance, such as Bucher's "confession" in which he professed to "paean" (pee on) the North Koreans; such as the photograph of the crew with raised middle fingers, which they described to their captors as the "Hawaiian good luck salute." This defiance earned them even more intense beatings.

The U.S. Navy, in its infinite wisdom, convened a court of inquiry, which recommended that the senior officers of the *Pueblo* face a court martial. In a rare display of compassion, Secretary of the Navy John Chafee rejected the recommendation, saying "They have suffered enough." And still, POW medals were not awarded the crew until 1990, 22 years later.

All things considered, one would have hoped for a *mea culpa* or two from the very top of the leadership ranks—the Secretary of the Navy, the Secretary of Defense, or the Commander in Chief himself. Something like this:

> I made a mistake. I sent the USS Pueblo into hostile waters, loaded with sensitive material and equipment, virtually unarmed and unprotected, with no contingency plan in the event of an attack. This mistake came at a horrendous cost to the crew, their families, and the security of our nation as a whole. For this, I offer my sincere and most profound apology.

Of course, no such statement has ever been forthcoming. Whatever happened to *The Buck Stops Here*? Where are men like Harry Truman when we really need them?

Tuesday, December 24

S KIP TOOK THE PHONE CALL in his office where he was busy
writing out checks, paying all the bills that were due.

"Hello."

"Hi, Skip, this is Aaron at the janitorial service."

"Hi, Aaron. What's up?"

"I'm afraid I've got some bad news."

"Yeah?"

"Remember Thaddeus Brown? He used to be on your account,
with Bobbie Washington."

"Yeah, of course. He was drafted into the Army. Great kid,
and a hard worker."

"Right, Skip. Here's the thing: we got word today that Thad
was killed in Vietnam." Aaron waited several seconds for Skip to
respond. "Skip?"

"I heard you, Aaron." Skip was thinking back to that night
in March when LBJ said he would not run for re-election,
remembering Thad's words: *Where does that leave the rest of us?*

"Anyway, I wanted to let you know that Bobbie won't be in
tonight. You know she and Thad were related—cousins, I think.
I'm trying to line up someone to fill in for her." There was another
long pause. "Skip?"

"Yeah, okay . . . look, Aaron, let's just cancel the service for
tonight. I think we'll close up early. Everybody wants to be home
with family tonight anyway. We'll pick it up on Thursday, after
Christmas. Okay?"

"Okay, Skip. We'll have our crew there on Thursday night. Thanks." With that, he hung up.

Skip sat looking at the phone. *Where does that leave the rest of us?* The words played over in his head. Well . . . now Thaddeus Brown had his answer.

The lights were burning brightly in the Browns' home, a small wood frame bungalow in a predominantly black neighborhood. The Washington family came through the front door to wails of grief from Thad's parents and siblings. They hugged and cried and tried to console the family, and just as calm was being restored, a new set of friends or relatives would come through the door and the heartbreaking scene would be repeated.

A beautifully decorated Christmas tree stood in the front window. No one could bear to turn on the lights that had been strung so lovingly, and the tree stood there as a sad reminder of the season, brightly wrapped packages arrayed around the base.

Bobbie Washington was devastated. She loved Thad and had always looked up to him, as though he were an older and wiser brother. She could not accept the fact that he was dead, his life blown away in some God-forsaken jungle half way around the world. She thought of all the time they had spent together growing up. She could still see him as that mischievous little boy, teasing her, making her laugh so hard that her sides hurt. And she remembered the way he comforted her on the night Dr. King was assassinated. It was almost more than she could bear.

They had been at the Browns' for nearly an hour and the house was packed now with family and friends. Bobbie began to think about Johnny Harris. She longed to have him wrap her in his arms, to hold her and tell her she would come through this, that in time her heart would heal, to feel his love for her one more time. She knew it would not be fair, that she had done the right thing by breaking up with him, setting him free to move on with the life he was intended to live. And yet, she could not help herself. She could almost feel his arms around her. All it would take was a simple phone call, just seven little digits. If she reached out to him, she knew he would come to her. She went to the phone sitting on the little table in the hall, picked up the receiver and began to dial.

Just then, her brother Lucas came down the hall on his way to the bathroom. "Hey, what's goin' on? Who are you calling?" Their eyes locked for a moment and he knew the answer. "Don't, Bobbie . . . don't do it . . . leave him be . . . you did the right thing, don't mess it up now." He saw her face begin to crumble and he took the receiver from her gently and placed it back on the cradle, at the same time gathering her into his arms. She buried her head against his chest and began to cry.

Ellamae Brown had taken over the kitchen as soon as she arrived. Friends and family came bearing heaping plates of food—fried chicken, sliced ham, meatloaf, cookies, cakes and pies of every flavor—and she took it all in hand, organizing the dishes, placing the food on the dining room table where people could help themselves. She latched on to volunteers and sent them about collecting dirty dishes and utensils, set others to washing and drying them, then back to the table to be used again. It was her strength. And it protected her from her grief. Busy hands were her best defense.

As things began to settle down, she put down her dishtowel and her apron and started down the hall toward the bathroom. She saw Lucas and Bobbie standing near the phone, Lucas attempting to console his sister as she sobbed against his chest. Ellamae stopped to offer her own words of comfort.

"There now, child . . . that's it . . . just let it go . . . let it all out. Sweet Jesus, comfort this child." Then she added: "Amen."

Across town, the Harrises were holding their traditional Christmas Eve open house. The lights of the tree burned brightly in the front window, inviting all to come inside where it was warm. The dining room table was loaded with treats and Big John Harris had whipped up a batch of his famous Tom 'n Jerry batter. As people arrived at the door, Martha would greet them warmly and take their coats and John would hand them a frothy, steaming T&J. The aroma of cinnamon, cloves, and nutmeg—not to mention the rum and brandy—hung in the air as John delivered his standard warning: "Watch out, cause this is a man's drink, a *real* man's drink!"

Most of the guests had seen, heard and tasted this all before, but the Hashimotos, being new to the neighborhood, were first-timers. Kenji took a sip of the potent drink and raised his eyebrows. "Wow! It's a good thing we don't have to drive home." Tami decided that Big John was right: it was a man's drink and she could do without it, except perhaps to warm her hands.

Eric looked around for John Jr., asked Mrs. Harris where to find him, and was directed to his bedroom, just down the hall. He knocked firmly on the door and heard Johnny say, "Come on in." Eric looked around the room as he entered: a full-size bed, a dresser, a bedside table, a desk and a chair, all neatly arranged to maximize the space. The walls were adorned with posters of John's favorite athletes: Bart Starr, Willie Mays, Bill Russell, and Jim Otto. John turned to face him and Eric saw that he was wearing khaki pants and a navy blue sweatshirt with "UCLA" in large gold letters across the front.

"Hey, Eric. Merry Christmas."

"Same to you, Johnny. Nice sweatshirt, man."

"Yeah, my dad insisted that I wear it. Go Bruins!"

It registered with Eric that John's words were slurred. He looked to the bedside table and saw the cream colored mug with the gold-leaf lettering that read "Tom 'n Jerry." He wondered how many John had consumed. John came across the room toward Eric now and wrapped him in a backslapping bear hug. Eric could smell the alcohol on his breath. They each took a step back, but John continued to grip Eric's shirt at the shoulders, as though he was afraid to let go.

"Doing some celebrating tonight, eh?"

"Yeah, I had a couple. You should try one. My dad loves making them."

"I'll pass, thanks. Hey, John, you okay?"

"Yeah—"

"You sure? You look like hell." Eric was being blunt, and honest.

"I'm okay." John was still gripping his shirt, staring directly into his eyes, and Eric could see that he was tearing up. "Ah shit, Eric . . . shit . . . it's no good, man . . . it's no damn good."

"What, Johnny? What is it?"

"It's no good without her, man . . . no damn good . . . nothing's worth a shit without her."

Eric had no idea what John was talking about. No good without *her*? Who the hell is *she*? He didn't know that John was involved with anyone. He eased John back a couple of steps so that he could sit down on the bed, where he promptly planted his elbows on his knees and buried his face in his hands, sniffling loudly every so often. Eric stood in front of him, embarrassed and confused. He caught his reflection in the mirrored doors of the closet and saw a look of mild panic on his face. He glanced toward the door and felt the urge to make a run for it. But he couldn't bring himself to do it.

He thought back to his first days at Vallejo High when he'd felt so totally alone and lost. Then John Harris was there, showing him around the sprawling campus, introducing him to his friends, sitting with him in the cafeteria, making sure he was included. Eric knew he couldn't walk away now. It was time to step up, time to be a friend. He reached for the chair in front of the desk and pulled it over. He sat in front of John and gripped his wrists, pulling his hands away from his face. A pathetic little trickle of snot ran down John's upper lip.

Eric reached for a tissue from the box on the bedside table and handed it to John who blew his nose loudly. "Okay," he said. "Talk to me, man. It's no good without who?"

Skip and Marty sat on the couch in the front room of their home, watching the images flicker on the television screen. It felt a little strange to be home so early, to close up the bar on a night when business was generally pretty good. But they knew it was the right decision. Neither one of them had the heart to soldier on with the news of Thaddeus Brown's death weighing them down.

They were watching a special broadcast from space, the *Apollo 8* astronauts beaming back words and images from lunar orbit. The pictures of the Moon's surface were stark and amazing, but it was the view of the Earth, a shinning blue and white marble set in the blackness of space that was awe inspiring. Then the astronauts took turns speaking:

William Anders:
For all the people on Earth, the crew of *Apollo 8* has a message we would like to send to you:

In the beginning God created the heaven and the earth. And the earth was without form, and void; and darkness was upon the face of the deep. And the Spirit of God moved upon the face of the waters. And God said, Let there be light; and there was light. And God saw the light, that it was good; and God divided the light from the darkness.

Jim Lovell:
And God called the light Day, and the darkness he called Night. And the evening and the morning were the first day. And God said, Let there be a firmament in the midst of the waters, and let it divide the waters from the waters. And God made the firmament, and it divided the waters which were under the firmament from the waters which were above the firmament; and it was so. And God called the firmament Heaven. And the evening and the morning were the second day.

Frank Borman:
And God said, Let the waters under the heavens be gathered together unto one place, and let the dry land

> appear; and it was so. And God called the dry land
> Earth; and the gathering together of the waters called he
> the Seas; and God saw that it was good.

> Borman closed the broadcast: And from the crew of
> *Apollo 8*, we close with good night, good luck, a Merry
> Christmas, and God bless all of you—all of you on the
> good Earth.

Skip and Marty looked at one another, tears streaming down their faces, and reached out to join hands. They cried for the beauty of the words from Genesis, sacred to Jews and Christians all around the world. They cried for Thad Brown, like a thousand other young soldiers, making his way home in a flag-draped coffin. They cried for Martin Luther King and Bobby Kennedy, and everything else that had happened in this rotten bull-bitch of a year, 1968. Thank God it was finally coming to a close.

New Year's Eve, 1968

T HEY GATHERED AROUND THE TELEVISION screen, watching the lighted ball drop in Times Square. "Five . . . four . . . three . . . two . . . one . . . Happy New Year!" Once again, the lucky ones turned to that special someone and shared a kiss.

"Happy New Year. I love you."

"I love you too."

"I wonder what this year will bring? All good things, I hope."

"Hey, you said that last year and look what happened."

"Ouch! You got that right. Let's hope for a quiet year, one we can all forget."

"God knows we need a break. And you know what? This party is a bore. You know what I'd like to do?"

"What's that?"

"Go home, take off our clothes . . ."

". . . and get in a pile. Great idea! We'll make it a New Year's tradition."

"I'll get our coats and we'll say goodbye."

No question about it, 1968 delivered more than its share of Significant Emotional Events, enough to impact every family in our story. But did these events leave any lasting changes? Were any lenses altered?

Let's consider Kenji Hashimoto. More than twenty years after the end of World War II, a war in which he served with distinction, he is turned away from a barbershop because ". . . we remember Pearl Harbor." In spite of a budding friendship with John Harris,

115

how does Kenji see the curly-haired, round-eyed population that dominates his world?

Then there is Isaac Washington, a man who worked hard to achieve his dream of becoming a registered nurse. And yet he still must deal with being stopped by the police for DWB (driving while black). Did his view of white folks change in the course of this year?

And finally, there is John Harris, Sr., a man with definite views about certain people. Were his beliefs about Japanese-Americans changed in any way by getting to know Kenji Hashimoto? When Isaac Washington caused that little section of hot dog to be dislodged from Jenny's throat, did it change the way John viewed African-Americans? And even if John's lens was changed forever, what would he see if John Jr. and Bobbie stood before him, holding hands?

Maybe all we can say for sure is this: that it is a long way from where we are to where we should be; that the American dream we share is greater than the bigotry we've learned; that—like it or not—we're all in this together; and that we all look at the world through an imperfect lens, a work in progress for a lifetime.

As Ellamae Brown might add: *God, watch over these good people and keep them from harm.*

And let us all say Amen!

Acknowledgements

I WOULD LIKE TO EXPRESS my heart-felt thanks to some very special people who played an important role in the development of this novel.

I am blessed with two wonderful friends, **Carolyn Vecchio Brown** and **Tom Campbell**, who are always willing to act as my first readers. Both of them read an early version of '68 and their comments were invaluable. In addition, they are the world's greatest cheerleaders, always pushing me forward with their generous remarks.

It was a great feeling to know that my son **Matt Spooner** would read each new set of chapters and provide an encouraging comment or two, in addition to content and editing advice upon request. My sister-in-law **Linda Yassinger** was also a loyal reader. My work was never finished until I heard from Matt and Linda.

My son-in-law **Cliff Hoecker**, an officer in the Gresham, Oregon, police department, provided background and advice regarding the procedure for conducting routine—and not so routine—traffic stops.

Linda Etheridge Rich, who has authored three novels of her own—and is hard at work on a fourth—read an early version of '68 and provided suggestions that made it a much better product.

Finally, there is **Harry Diavatis**, publisher of the *Monday Update*, who gives me free reign to publish my work in his fine weekly newsletter. Harry, thanks for the soapbox and the megaphone.

So now it's back to the keyboard. For me, writing is a compulsion; having an audience is a blessing. Thank you for reading.